PENGUIN BOOKS

First Love and Other Novellas

Samuel Beckett was born in Dublin in 1906. After graduating from Trinity College, Dublin, in the late twenties he went to Paris to join the staff of the École Normale Supérieure. He very soon made the acquaintance of James Joyce and his first published work was an essay on Joyce's *Work in Progress* (later *Finnegan's Wake*). This was soon followed by an award-winning long poem, *Whoroscope*, and a critical monograph titled *Proust*. He briefly held a lectureship in French at Trinity College, but resigned from the post when he realized he was unsuited to teaching. A novel written in the early thirties (*Dream of Fair to Middling Women*, published posthumously in 1992) was recast as a set of linked short stories and appeared as *More Pricks than Kicks* in 1934. A collection of poems, *Echo's Bones and Other Precipitates*, appeared in 1935, and was followed by the novel *Murphy* in 1938. He had settled in Paris in 1937 following extensive travels in Germany and a lengthy period undergoing psychotherapy in London. He remained in France during the Second World War and was active in the French Resistance. The novel *Watt* was written at this time, but was not published until 1953. After the liberation of France he returned to Dublin to visit his mother whom he had not seen for some years, but soon returned to France as a storekeeper and interpreter with the Irish Red Cross and served in their hospital in Saint-Lô. From the spring of 1946 he elected to use French as his language of literary composition and, over the next five years, wrote two plays, four novels, poetry, criticism and four novellas in that language. With the production of *En attendant Godot (Waiting for Godot)* in 1953, Beckett was finally recognized as a great artist. Successful productions of the play in Berlin, London, Dublin and New York consolidated his reputation. During his subsequent career as playwright and novelist in both French and English he redefined the artistic possibilities of writing for the theatre and of prose fiction. Samuel Beckett won the Prix Formentor in 1961 and the Nobel Prize for Literature in 1969.

He died in Paris in December 1989 and is buried in Montparnasse.

Gerry Dukes lectures in literature at Mary Immaculate College, University of Limerick. His stage adaptation, with the actor Barry McGovern, of Beckett's post-war trilogy of novels as 'I'll go on' has played around the world. He has published essays, reviews and articles on modern Irish writing and visual art in Europe and the United States. He currently lives in Dublin.

SAMUEL BECKETT

First Love and Other Novellas

Edited and with an Introduction and Notes by Gerry Dukes

PENGUIN BOOKS

PENGUIN BOOKS

Published by the Penguin Group
Penguin Books Ltd, 80 Strand, London WC2R 0RL, England
Penguin Putnam Inc., 375 Hudson Street, New York, New York 10014, USA
Penguin Books Australia Ltd, 250 Camberwell Road, Camberwell, Victoria 3124, Australia
Penguin Books Canada Ltd, 10 Alcorn Avenue, Toronto, Ontario, Canada M4V 3B2
Penguin Books India (P) Ltd, 11 Community Centre, Panchsheel Park, New Delhi – 110 017, India
Penguin Books (NZ) Ltd, Cnr Rosedale and Airborne Roads, Albany, Auckland, New Zealand
Penguin Books (South Africa) (Pty) Ltd, 24 Sturdee Avenue, Rosebank 2196, South Africa

Penguin Books Ltd, Registered Offices: 80 Strand, London WC2R 0RL, England

www.penguin.com

This collection first published in Great Britain as *Four Novellas* by John Calder 1977
Published as *The Expelled and Other Novellas* in Penguin Books 1980
This edition published with an Introduction and editorial matter 2000

10

Set in 10.75/13.75 pt PostScript Granjon
Typeset by Rowland Phototypesetting Ltd, Bury St Edmunds, Suffolk
Printed in Great Britain by Clays Ltd, St Ives plc

ISBN-13: 978–0–141–18015–1
ISBN-10: 0–141–18015–3

Contents

Introduction

These four novellas are amongst the first substantial fruits of Beckett's transfer to French as his language of literary composition. Having left the Irish Red Cross hospital in the Normandy town of Saint-Lô when his contract came to an end in January 1946, Beckett returned to Paris and within a month had embarked on what he later called 'a frenzy of writing'. Between February and December 1946 he wrote the four novellas and the novel *Mercier et Camier*. James Knowlson, in his indispensable biography,[1] has established a chronology of composition running thus: *Suite* (later *La Fin*) written from mid-February to May; *Mercier et Camier* between July and October; *L'Expulsé* during October; *Premier Amour* from October to December and *Le Calmant* in December.

The novellas are unprecedented in the canon of Beckett's prose fiction for at least two reasons: they were written in French and each novella is presented as a first-person narrative. Beckett had worked with his friend Alfred Péron on translating Joyce's *Anna Livia Plurabelle* in 1930 and on his own novel *Murphy* (published in English in 1938) into French, and he had also written some poetry and sundry prose pieces in that language. The novellas (and *Mercier et Camier*), however, constitute his first extended use of French as the language of composition. It is worth bearing in mind that by 1946 Beckett was in his tenth year of residence in France and that for much of that time his daily life had been almost exclusively francophone. There is a great gap between conversational and literary registers in most languages but for a superb linguist like Beckett with a fine academic training it is probable the gap could be readily bridged.

Beckett was no doubt assisted in bridging the gap by casting his novellas as first-person narratives. The novellas come to us as 'spoken' utterances; they mimic speech. This is not to suggest that the texture of the novellas is in any way bereft of Beckett's well-established signature effects – rhetorical shapeliness, arcane reference, literary allusion – but that these effects are suspended within a medium that looks and sounds innocent of 'literature'. Consider how Dante's *Inferno* is invoked in this brief passage from *The Calmative*:

> But it was nothing, mere speechlessness due to long silence, as in the wood that darkens the mouth of hell, do you remember, I only just.[2]

Or how specialized physiological knowledge is deployed in this passage from *First Love*:

> Look, she said, stooping over her breasts, the haloes are darkening already. I summoned up my remaining strength and said, Abort, abort, and they'll blush like new.[3]

Such language procedures were to deliver rich dividends in the immediate future when Beckett came to write *En attendant Godot* and the novels of the so-called trilogy.

Beckett's earlier, English language fictions, however experimental they may have appeared, still had recourse to the traditional elements of plot, character and recognizable settings such as Dublin – city and county – and the city of London. In the transfer to first-person narratives, in which the narrators are endowed with only vague notions of where they happen to be, the necessity to designate specific locations evaporates but traces of specificity remain. Irish readers need no further clues as to the settings of the novellas: mountains to the south, a great bay with flashing beacons and a lightship, a city – with two canals – built at the mouth of a river. The inevitable conclusion is that the events, in general, are set in Dublin and environs. Beckett, however, generates ambiguities by complicating matters. In *The End* the narrator is discharged from an institution of some kind and sets off, in the evening, towards the city. He passes through areas he fails to recognize but concedes that 'the general impression was the same as before'. He heads south:

By keeping the red part of the sky as much as possible on my right hand I came at last to the river. Here all seemed at first sight more or less as I had left it. But if I had looked more closely I would doubtless have discovered many changes. And indeed I subsequently did so. But the general appearance of the river, flowing between its quays and under its bridges, had not changed. Yes, the river still gave the impression it was flowing in the wrong direction.[4]

Beckett performs here a kind of double exposure or montage in which he superimposes Paris and the river Seine on Dublin and the river Liffey, as if the landscape were being viewed by the strabismic gaze of Lulu/Anna from *First Love*. Again in *The End*, when the narrator reaches the decayed cabin in the mountains he finds the floor

strewn with excrements, both human and animal, with condoms and vomit. In a cowpad a heart had been traced, pierced by an arrow. And yet there was nothing to attract tourists.[5]

This is in direct contrast to *First Love* where the narrator, who has taken refuge in a deserted cowshed in a field, singles out the scant population of his country as one of its charms while noting that this demographic result is obtained 'without help of the meanest contraceptive'. Readers conversant with the social and economic history of Ireland in the 1930s will have no difficulty in recognizing this rural landscape of *First Love* as Ireland, denuded of much of its population by the collapse of agricultural prices precipitated by the economic war with Britain. One of the refuges, then, is specifically Irish.

Throughout the four novellas various references – to the sounds of the stone-cutters' hammers, to the gorse fires on the hills, to displays of public piety – conspire to localize the texts in distinctively Irish contexts. Even the odd name of the lawyer Mr Nidder in *The Expelled* resolves itself when reversed into Reddin, a common Irish surname, as is Ward, who is named as the previous owner of the narrator's copy of Geulincx's *Ethics* in *The End*. In that novella the narrator recalls:

> I heard faintly the cries of the gulls ravening about the mouth of the sewer near by. In a spew of yellow foam, if my memory serves me right, the filth gushed into the river and the slush of birds above screaming with hunger and fury.[6]

The wording of Beckett's translation at this point recalls his earlier poem 'Enueg I':

> Blotches of doomed yellow in the pit of the Liffey;
> The fingers of the ladders hooked over the parapet,
> Soliciting;
> A slush of vigilant gulls in the grey spew of the sewer.[7]

There are locational counter-indications in the texts as well: a horse-butcher's shop, boulevards, a charming Saxon Stützenwechsel on a church, the Ohlsdorf graveyard, the Lüneburg heath. There is no need to labour these antinomies because, as the narrator in *The Calmative* informs us, 'we are needless to say in a skull'.[8] The landscapes of the novellas are the landscapes of memory, composite places of superimpositions and elisions.

Translations are acts of superimposition and elision too – and they offer opportunities for substantial revisions and rewrites, as do successive editions. Of the novellas, the case of *The End* is the most complicated. It was begun in English under the title *Suite* but finished in French. A truncated French version was published in *Temps modernes* in July 1946. In 1954 Beckett worked with Richard Seaver on a translation of the novella which appeared in the magazine *Merlin*. The text's next appearance in English was in *Evergreen Review* in 1960. Beckett entirely reworked the translation for this appearance but, with typical magnanimity, he retained the acknowledgement of Seaver's collaboration.

Collaboration with Richard Seaver on the translation of *The Expelled* is similarly acknowledged, even though Beckett reworked the translation for first English publication in *Evergreen Review* in 1962. Beckett completed the translation of *The Calmative* in September 1966 for its first publication in *Evergreen Review* in 1967, and completed the translation of *First Love* in February 1973.

This new edition of the novellas has the simple objective of providing accurate reading texts – in so far as such a thing is possible in the present state of Beckett scholarship. The provision of accurate reading texts arises ineluctably from the modalities of publication of the texts. In the case of *First Love*, to take the simplest example, it is evident from the pre-publication documentary record that Beckett produced two 'final texts': one for American publication and one for the British market. In each case Beckett made corrections and revisions at the proof stage but he did not necessarily apply the same corrections and revisions to the two sets of proofs.

This resulted in slight but significant divergences between the American and British texts. Despite the dates of first publication of the two texts (1974 for Grove Press and 1973 for Calder & Boyars) the corrections and revisions to the British edition post-date those to the American. Therefore the British first edition must be regarded as Beckett's final 'final text'.

Inevitably, because authors and compositors are human (the same goes for editors), slippage can and does occur; publishing is not yet an error-free zone. In the Notes which follow the texts here printed, some of these slippages are noted, along with other matters which might be of assistance to readers. The Notes have been kept to a minimum so as not to distract the reader from the texts themselves.

I would like to express my gratitude to the Steering Committee of the Board of Governors of Mary Immaculate College, University of Limerick, for a semester's relief from teaching during which some of the work on this edition was performed. My thanks are also due to Professor Breon Mitchell of Bloomington, Indiana, who responded most comprehensively to my occasional bibliographical inquiries; to both Anne Posega of the Olin Library at the Washington University, St Louis and Kathleen Manwaring of the Department of Special Collections at Syracuse University Library for providing copies of essential pre-publication documents (itemized in the Notes); to Michael Bott at the library of the University of Reading for making my visit there both pleasurable and rewarding; to Glenn Horowitz in New York for providing copies of corrected proofs for Beckett's *Collected Shorter Prose 1945–1980* in his possession.

For permission to cite copyright materials I thank M. Jérome Lindon, literary executor of the Beckett Estate. For vigilant reading and rescue from error my thanks go to Barry

McGovern, that consummate interpreter of Beckett's work, on and off stage. Paul Keegan (formerly of Penguin) initiated the project and I thank him for his confidence and tolerance of delay: he was ably followed at Penguin by Anna South, who applied gentle pressure when it was needed.

Gerry Dukes
Dublin 1999

Notes

1. *Damned to Fame: The Life of Samuel Beckett* (1996). See especially Chapter 15.
2. In *Le Calmant*: *Mais ce n'était rien, rien que l'aphonie due au long silence, comme dans le bosquet où s'ouvrent les enfers, vous rappelez-vous, moi tout juste.*
3. In *Premier Amour*: *Regardez dit-elle, se courbant sur ses seins, l'auréole fonce déjà. Je rassemblai mes dernières forces et lui dis, Avortez, avortez, comme ça elle ne foncera plus.*
4. In *La Fin*: *A force de garder le côté rouge du ciel autant que possible à ma droite j'arrivai enfin au fleuve. Là tout semblait, à première vue, plus ou moins tel que je l'avais laissé. Mais en y regardant de plus près j'aurais découvert bien de changements sans doute. C'est ce que je fis plus tard. Mais l'aspect général du fleuve, coulant entre ses quais et sous ses ponts, n'avait pas changé. Le fleuve notamment me donnait l'impression, comme toujours, de couler dans le mauvais sens.*
5. In *La Fin*: *Des excréments jonchaient le sol, d'homme, de vache, de chien, ainsi que des préservatifs et des vomissures. Dans une bouse, on avait tracé un coeur, percé d'une flèche. Ce n'était pourtant pas un site classé.*
6. In *La Fin*: *J'entendais sourdement les cries des mouettes qui s'affairaient tout près, autour de la bouche des égouts. Dans un bouillonnement jaunâtre, si j'avais bonne mémoire, les immondices s'unissaient au fleuve, les oiseaux tourbillonnaient au-dessus, en brailland de faim et de colère.*
7. *Poems in English* (Calder & Boyars, London, 1961). 'Enueg I' was

written in the autumn of 1930 and first collected in *Echo's Bones* (1935). Joyce incorporated a similar memory into the text of *Ulysses*: *From its sluice in Wood quay wall under Tom Devan's office Poddle river hung out in fealty a tongue of liquid sewage. Ulysses*, edited with an Introduction by Jeri Johnson (Oxford University Press, 1993), p. 242.

8. In *Le Calmant*: *nous sommes bien entendu dans une tête.*

The End

They clothed me and gave me money. I knew what the money was for, it was to get me started. When it was gone I would have to get more, if I wanted to go on. The same for the shoes, when they were worn out I would have to get them mended, or get myself another pair, or go on barefoot, if I wanted to go on. The same for the coat and trousers, needless to say, with this difference, that I could go on in my shirtsleeves, if I wanted. The clothes – shoes, socks, trousers, shirt, coat, hat – were not new, but the deceased must have been about my size. That is to say, he must have been a little shorter, a little thinner, for the clothes did not fit me so well in the beginning as they did at the end, the shirt especially, and it was many a long day before I could button it at the neck, or profit by the collar that went with it, or pin the tails together between my legs in the way my mother had taught me. He must have put on his Sunday best to go to the consultation, perhaps for the first time, unable to bear it any longer. Be that as it may the hat was a bowler, in good shape. I said, Keep your hat and give me back mine. I added, Give me back my greatcoat. They replied that they had burnt them, together with my other clothes. I understood then that the end was near, at least fairly near. Later on I tried to exchange this hat for a cap, or a slouch which could be pulled down over my face, but without much success. And yet I could not go about bare-headed, with my skull in the state it was. At first this hat was too small, then it got used to me. They gave me a tie, after long discussion. It seemed a pretty tie to me, but I didn't like it. When it came at last I was too tired to send it back. But in the end it came in useful. It was blue, with kinds of little stars. I didn't feel well, but they told me I was well enough. They didn't say in so many words that I was as well as I would ever be, but that was the implication. I lay inert on the bed and it took three women to put on my trousers. They didn't seem to take much interest in my private parts which to tell the truth were nothing to write home about, I didn't take much interest in them myself. But they might have passed some remark. When they had finished I got up and finished dressing unaided. They told me to sit on the bed and wait. All the bedding had disappeared. It made me angry that they had not let me wait in the familiar bed, instead of leaving me standing in the cold, in these clothes that smelt of sulphur. I said, You might have left me in the bed till the last moment. Men all in white came in with mallets in their hands. They dismantled the bed and took away the pieces. One of the women followed them out and came back with a chair which she set before me. I had done well to pretend I was angry. But to make it quite clear to them how angry I was that they had not left me in my bed I gave the chair a kick that sent it flying. A man came in and made a sign to me to follow him. In the hall he gave me a paper to sign. What's this, I said, a safe-conduct? It's a receipt, he said, for the clothes and money you have received. What money? I said. It was then I received the money. To think I had almost departed without a penny in my pocket. The sum was not large, compared to other sums, but to me it seemed large. I saw the familiar objects, companions of so many bearable hours. The stool, for example, dearest of all. The long afternoons together, waiting for it to be time for bed. At times I felt its wooden life invade me, till I myself became a piece of old wood. There was even a hole for my cyst. Then the window pane with the patch of frosting gone, where I used to press my eye in the hour of need, and rarely in vain. I am greatly obliged to you, I said, is there a law which prevents you from throwing me out naked and penniless? That would damage our reputation in the long run, he replied. Could they not possibly keep me a little longer, I said, I could make myself useful. Useful, he said, joking apart you would be willing to make yourself useful? A moment later he went on, If they believed you were really willing to make yourself useful they would keep you, I am sure. The number of times I had said I was going to make myself useful, I wasn't going to start that again. How weak I felt! Perhaps, I said, they would consent to take back the money and keep me a little longer. This is a charitable institution, he said, and the money is a gift you receive when you leave. When it is gone you will have to get more, if you want to go on. Never come back here whatever you do, you would not be let in. Don't go to any of our branches either, they would turn you away. Exelmans! I cried. Come come, he said, and anyway no one understands a tenth of what you say. I'm so old, I said. You are not so old as all that, he said. May I stay here just a little longer, I said, till the rain is over? You may wait in the cloister, he said, the rain will go on all day. You may wait in the cloister till six o'clock, you will hear the bell. If anyone challenges you, you need only say you have permission to shelter in the cloister. Whose name will I give? I said. Weir, he said.

I had not been long in the cloister when the rain stopped and the sun came out. It was low and I reckoned it must be getting on for six, considering the season. I stayed there looking through the archway at the sun as it went down behind the cloister. A man appeared and asked me what I was doing.

What do you want? were the words he used. Very friendly. I replied that I had Mr Weir's permission to stay in the cloister till six o'clock. He went away, but came back immediately. He must have spoken to Mr Weir in the interim, for he said, You must not loiter in the cloister now the rain is over.

Now I was making my way through the garden. There was that strange light which follows a day of persistent rain, when the sun comes out and the sky clears too late to be of any use. The earth makes a sound as of sighs and the last drops fall from the emptied cloudless sky. A small boy, stretching out his hands and looking up at the blue sky, asked his mother how such a thing was possible. Fuck off, she said. I suddenly remembered I had not thought of asking Mr Weir for a piece of bread. He would surely have given it to me. I had as a matter of fact thought of it during our conversation in the hall, I had said to myself, Let us first finish our conversation, then I'll ask. I knew well they would not keep me. I would gladly have turned back, but I was afraid one of the guards would stop me and tell me I would never see Mr Weir again. That might have added to my sorrow. And anyway I never turned back on such occasions.

In the street I was lost. I had not set foot in this part of the city for a long time and it seemed greatly changed. Whole buildings had disappeared, the palings had changed position, and on all sides I saw, in great letters, the names of tradesmen I had never seen before and would have been at a loss to pronounce. There were streets where I remembered none, some I did remember had vanished and others had completely changed their names. The general impression was the same as before. It is true I did not know the city very well. Perhaps it was quite a different one. I did not know where I was supposed to be going. I had the great good fortune, more than once, not to be run over. My appearance still made people laugh, with that hearty jovial laugh so good for the health. By keeping the red part of the sky as much as possible on my right hand I came at last to the river. Here all seemed at first sight more or less as I had left it. But if I had looked more closely I would doubtless have discovered many changes. And indeed I subsequently did so. But the general appearance of the river, flowing between its quays and under its bridges, had not changed. Yes, the river still gave the impression it was flowing in the wrong direction. That's all a pack of lies I feel. My bench was still there. It was shaped to fit the curves of the seated body. It stood beside a watering trough, gift of a Mrs Maxwell to the city horses, according to the inscription. During the short time I rested there several horses took advantage of this monument. The iron shoes approached and the jingle of the harness. Then silence. That was the horse looking at me. Then the noise of pebbles and mud that horses make when drinking. Then the silence again. That was the horse looking at me again. Then the pebbles again. Then the silence again. Till the horse had finished drinking or the driver deemed it had drunk its fill. The horses were uneasy. Once, when the noise stopped, I turned and saw the horse looking at me. The driver too was looking at me. Mrs Maxwell would have been pleased if she could have seen her trough rendering such services to the city horses. When it was night, after a tedious twilight, I took off my hat which was paining me. I longed to be under cover again, in an empty place, close and warm, with artificial light, an oil lamp for choice, with a pink shade for preference. From time to time someone would come to make sure I was all right and needed nothing. It was long since I had longed for anything and the effect on me was horrible.

In the days that followed I visited several lodgings, without much success. They usually slammed the door in my face, even when I showed my money and offered to pay a week in advance, or even two. It was in vain I put on my best manners, smiled and spoke distinctly, they slammed the door in my face before I could even finish my little speech. It was at this time I perfected a method of doffing my hat at once courteous and discreet, neither servile nor insolent. I slipped it smartly forward, held it a second poised in such a way that the person addressed could not see my skull, then slipped it back. To do that naturally, without creating an unfavourable impression, is no easy matter. When I deemed that to tip my hat would suffice, I naturally did no more than tip it. But to tip one's hat is no easy matter either. I subsequently solved this problem, always fundamental in time of adversity, by wearing a kepi and saluting in military fashion, no, that must be wrong, I don't know, I had my hat at the end. I never made the mistake of wearing medals. Some landladies were in such need of money that they let me in immediately and showed me the room. But I couldn't come to an agreement with any of them. Finally I found a basement. With this woman I came to an agreement at once. My oddities, that's the expression she used, did not alarm her. She nevertheless insisted on making the bed and cleaning the room once a week, instead of once a month as I requested. She told me that while she was cleaning, which would not take long, I could wait in the area. She added, with a great deal of feeling, that she would never put me out in bad weather. This woman was Greek, I think, or Turkish. She never spoke about herself. I somehow got the idea she was a widow or at least that her husband had left her. She had a strange accent. But so had I with my way of assimilating the vowels and omitting the consonants.

Now I didn't know where I was. I had a vague vision, not a real vision, I didn't see anything, of a big house five or six stories high, one of a block perhaps. It was dusk when I got there and I did not pay the same heed to my surroundings as I might have done if I had suspected they were to close about me. And by then I must have lost all hope. It is true that when I left this house it was a glorious day, but I never look back when leaving. I must have read somewhere, when I was small and still read, that it is better not to look back when leaving. And yet I sometimes did. But even without looking back it seems to me I should have seen something when leaving. But there it is. All I remember is my feet emerging from my shadow, one after the other. My shoes had stiffened and the sun brought out the cracks in the leather.

I was comfortable enough in this house, I must say. Apart from a few rats I was alone in the basement. The woman did her best to respect our agreement. About noon she brought me a big tray of food and took away the tray of the previous day. At the same time she brought me a clean chamber-pot. The chamber-pot had a large handle which she slipped over her arm, so that both her hands were free to carry the tray. The rest of the day I saw no more of her except sometimes when she peeped in to make sure nothing had happened to me. Fortunately I did not need affection. From my bed I saw the feet coming and going on the sidewalk. Certain evenings, when the weather was fine and I felt equal to it, I fetched my chair into the area and sat looking up into the skirts of the women passing by. Once I sent for a crocus bulb and planted it in the dark area, in an old pot. It must have been coming up to spring, it was probably not the right time for it. I left the pot outside, attached to a string I passed through the window. In the evening, when the weather was fine, a little light crept up the wall. Then I sat down beside the window and pulled on the string to keep the pot in the light and warmth. That can't have been easy, I don't see how I managed it. It was probably not the right thing for it. I manured it as best I could and pissed on it when the weather was dry. It may not have been the right thing for it. It sprouted, but never any flowers, just a wilting stem and a few chlorotic leaves. I would have liked to have a yellow crocus, or a hyacinth, but there, it was not to be. She wanted to take it away, but I told her to leave it. She wanted to buy me another, but I told her I didn't want another. What lacerated me most was the din of the newspaper boys. They went pounding by every day at the same hours, their heels thudding on the sidewalk, crying the names of their papers and even the headlines. The house noises disturbed me less. A little girl, unless it was a little boy, sang every evening at the same hour, somewhere above me. For a long time I could not catch the words. But hearing them day after day I finally managed to catch a few. Strange words for a little girl, or a little boy. Was it a song in my head or did it merely come from without? It was a sort of lullaby, I believe. It often sent me to sleep, even me. Sometimes it was a little girl who came. She had long red hair hanging down in two braids. I didn't know who she was. She lingered awhile in the room, then went away without a word. One day I had a visit from a policeman. He said I had to be watched, without explaining why. Suspicious, that was it, he told me I was suspicious. I let him talk. He didn't dare arrest me. Or perhaps he had a kind heart. A priest too, one day I had a visit from a priest. I informed him I belonged to a branch of the reformed church. He asked me what kind of clergyman I would like to see. Yes, there's that about the reformed church, you're lost, it's unavoidable. Perhaps he had a kind heart. He told me to let him know if I needed a helping hand. A helping hand! He gave me his name and explained where I could reach him. I should have made a note of it.

One day the woman made me an offer. She said she was in urgent need of cash and that if I could pay her six months in advance she would reduce my rent by one fourth during that period, something of that kind. This had the advantage of saving six weeks' (?) rent and the disadvantage of almost exhausting my small capital. But could you call that a disadvantage? Wouldn't I stay on in any case till my last penny was gone, and even longer, till she put me out? I gave her the money and she gave me a receipt.

One morning, not long after this transaction, I was awakened by a man shaking my shoulder. It could not have been much past eleven. He requested me to get up and leave his house immediately. He was most correct, I must say. His surprise, he said, was no less than mine. It was his house. His property. The Turkish woman had left the day before. But I saw her last night, I said. You must be mistaken, he said, for she brought the keys to my office no later than yesterday afternoon. But I just paid her six months' rent in advance, I said. Get a refund, he said. But I don't even know her name, I said, let alone her address. You don't know her name? he said. He must have thought I was lying. I'm sick, I said, I can't leave like this, without any notice. You're not so sick as all that, he said. He offered to send for a taxi, even an ambulance if I preferred. He said he needed the room immediately for his pig which even as he spoke was catching cold in a cart before the door and no one to look after him but a stray urchin whom he had never set eyes on before and who was probably busy tormenting him. I asked if he couldn't let me have another place, any old corner where I could lie down long enough to recover from the shock and decide what to do. He said he could not. Don't think I'm being unkind, he added. I could live here with the pig, I said, I'd look after him. The long months of peace, wiped out in an instant! Come now, come now, he said, get a grip on yourself, be a man, get up, that's enough. After all it was no concern of his. He had really been most patient. He must have visited the basement while I was sleeping.

I felt weak. Perhaps I was. I stumbled in the blinding light. A bus took me into the country. I sat down in a field in the sun. But it seems to me that was much later. I stuck leaves under my hat, all the way round, to make a shade. The night was cold. I wandered for hours in the fields. At last I found a heap of dung. The next day I started back to the city. They made me get off three buses. I sat down by the roadside and dried my clothes in the sun. I enjoyed doing that. I said to myself, There's nothing more to be done now, not a thing, till they are dry. When they were dry I brushed them with a brush, I think a kind of curry-comb, that I found in a stable. Stables have always been my salvation. Then I went to the house and begged a glass of milk and a slice of bread and butter. They gave me everything except the butter. May I rest in the stable? I said. No, they said. I still stank, but with a stink that pleased me. I much preferred it to my own which moreover it prevented me from smelling, except a waft now and then. In the days that followed I took the necessary steps to recover my money. I don't know exactly what happened, whether I couldn't find the address, or whether there was no such address, or whether the Greek woman was unknown there. I ransacked my pockets for the receipt, to try and decipher the name. It wasn't there. Perhaps she had taken it back while I was sleeping. I don't know how long I wandered thus, resting now in one place, now in another, in the city and in the country. The city had suffered many changes. Nor was the country as I remembered it. The general effect was the same. One day I caught sight of my son. He was striding along with a briefcase under his arm. He took off his hat and bowed and I saw he was as bald as a coot. I was almost certain it was he. I turned round to gaze after him. He went bustling along on his duck feet, bowing and scraping and flourishing his hat left and right. The insufferable son of a bitch.

One day I met a man I had known in former times. He lived in a cave by the sea. He had an ass that grazed winter and summer, over the cliffs, or along the little tracks leading down to the sea. When the weather was very bad this ass came down to the cave of his own accord and sheltered there till the storm was past. So they had spent many a night huddled together, while the wind howled and the sea pounded on the shore. With the help of this ass he could deliver sand, sea-wrack, and shells to the townsfolk, for their gardens. He couldn't carry much at a time, for the ass was old and small and the town was far. But in this way he earned a little money, enough to keep him in tobacco and matches and to buy a piece of bread from time to time. It was during one of these excursions that he met me, in the suburbs. He was delighted to see me, poor man. He begged me to go home with him and spend the night. Stay as long as you like, he said. What's wrong with your ass? I said. Don't mind him, he said, he doesn't know you. I reminded him that I wasn't in the habit of staying more than two or three minutes with anyone and that the sea did not agree with me. He seemed deeply grieved to hear it. So you won't come, he said. But to my amazement I got up on the ass and off we went, in the shade of the red chestnuts springing from the sidewalk. I held the ass by the mane, one hand in front of the other. The little boys jeered and threw stones, but their aim was poor, for they only hit me once, on the hat. A policeman stopped us and accused us of disturbing the peace. My friend replied that we were as nature had made us, the boys too were as nature had made them. It was inevitable, under these conditions, that the peace should be disturbed from time to time. Let us continue on our way, he said, and order will soon be restored throughout your beat. We followed the quiet, dustwhite inland roads with their hedges of hawthorn and fuchsia and their footpaths fringed with wild grass and daisies. Night fell. The ass carried me right to the mouth of the cave, for in the dark I could not have found my way down the path winding steeply to the sea. Then he climbed back to his pasture.

I don't know how long I stayed there. The cave was nicely arranged, I must say. I treated my crablice with salt water and seaweed, but a lot of nits must have survived. I put compresses of seaweed on my skull, which gave me great relief, but not for long. I lay in the cave and sometimes looked out at the horizon. I saw above me a vast trembling expanse without islands or promontories. At night a light shone into the cave at regular intervals. It was here I found the phial in my pocket. It was not broken, for the glass was not real glass. I thought Mr Weir had confiscated all my belongings. My host was out most of the time. He fed me on fish. It is easy for a man, a proper man, to live in a cave, far from everybody. He invited me to stay as long as I liked. If I preferred to be alone he would gladly prepare another cave for me further on. He would bring me food every day and drop in from time to time to make sure I was all right and needed nothing. He was kind. Unfortunately I did not need kindness. You wouldn't know of a lake dwelling? I said. I couldn't bear the sea, its splashing and heaving, its tides and general convulsiveness. The wind at least sometimes stops. My hands and feet felt as though they were full of ants. This kept me awake for hours on end. If I stayed here something awful would happen to me, I said, and a lot of good that would do me. You'd get drowned, he said. Yes, I said, or jump off the cliff. And to think I couldn't live anywhere else, he said, in my cabin in the mountains I was wretched. Your cabin in the mountains? I said. He repeated the story of his cabin in the mountains, I had forgotten it, it was as though I were hearing it for the first time. I asked him if he still had it. He replied he had not seen it since the day he fled from it, but that he believed it was still there, a little decayed no doubt. But when he urged me to take the key I refused, saying I had other plans. You will always find me here, he said, if you ever need me. Ah people. He gave me his knife.

What he called his cabin in the mountains was a sort of wooden shed. The door had been removed, for firewood, or for some other purpose. The glass had disappeared from the window. The roof had fallen in at several places. The interior was divided, by the remains of a partition, into two unequal parts. If there had been any furniture it was gone. The vilest acts had been committed on the ground and against the walls. The floor was strewn with excrements, both human and animal, with condoms and vomit. In a cowpad a heart had been traced, pierced by an arrow. And yet there was nothing to attract tourists. I noticed the remains of abandoned nosegays. They had been greedily gathered, carried for miles, then thrown away, because they were cumbersome or already withered. This was the dwelling to which I had been offered the key.

The scene was the familiar one of grandeur and desolation.

Nevertheless it was a roof over my head. I rested on a bed of ferns, gathered at great labour with my own hands. One day I couldn't get up. The cow saved me. Goaded by the icy mist she came in search of shelter. It was probably not the first time. She can't have seen me. I tried to suck her, without much success. Her udder was covered with dung. I took off my hat and, summoning all my energy, began to milk her into it. The milk fell to the ground and was lost, but I said to myself, No matter, it's free. She dragged me across the floor, stopping from time to time only to kick me. I didn't know our cows too could be so inhuman. She must have recently been milked. Clutching the dug with one hand I kept my hat under it with the other. But in the end she prevailed. For she dragged me across the threshold and out into the giant streaming ferns, where I was forced to let go.

As I drank the milk I reproached myself with what I had done. I could no longer count on this cow and she would warn the others. More master of myself I might have made a friend of her. She would have come every day, perhaps accompanied by other cows. I might have learnt to make butter, even cheese. But I said to myself, No, all is for the best.

Once on the road it was all downhill. Soon there were carts, but they all refused to take me up. In other clothes, with another face, they might have taken me up. I must have changed since my expulsion from the basement. The face notably seemed to have attained its climacteric. The humble, ingenuous smile would no longer come, nor the expression of candid misery, showing the stars and the distaff. I summoned them, but they would not come. A mask of dirty old hairy leather, with two holes and a slit, it was too far gone for the old trick of please your honour and God reward you and pity upon me. It was disastrous. What would I crawl with in future? I lay down on the side of the road and began to writhe each time I heard a cart approaching. That was so they would not think I was sleeping or resting. I tried to groan, Help! Help! But the tone that came out was that of polite conversation. My hour was not yet come and I could no longer groan. The last time I had cause to groan I had groaned as well as ever, and no heart within miles of me to melt. What was to become of me? I said to myself, I'll learn again. I lay down across the road at a narrow place, so that the carts could not pass without passing over my body, with one wheel at least, or two if there were four. But the day came when, looking round me, I was in the suburbs, and from there to the old haunts it was not far, beyond the stupid hope of rest or less pain.

So I covered the lower part of my face with a black rag and went and begged at a sunny corner. For it seemed to me my eyes were not completely spent, thanks perhaps to the dark glasses my tutor had given me. He had given me the *Ethics* of Geulincx. They were a man's glasses, I was a child. They found him dead, crumpled up in the water closet, his clothes in awful disorder, struck down by an infarctus. Ah what peace. The *Ethics* had his name (Ward) on the fly-leaf, the glasses had belonged to him. The bridge, at the time I am speaking of, was of brass wire, of the kind used to hang pictures and big mirrors, and two long black ribbons served as wings. I wound them round my ears and then down under my chin where I tied them together. The lenses had suffered, from rubbing in my pocket against each other and against the other objects there. I thought Mr Weir had confiscated all my belongings. But I had no further need of these glasses and used them merely to soften the glare of the sun. I should never have mentioned them. The rag gave me a lot of trouble. I got it in the end from the lining of my greatcoat, no, I had no greatcoat now, of my coat then. The result was a grey rag rather than a black, perhaps even chequered, but I had to make do with it. Till afternoon I held my face raised towards the southern sky, then towards the western till night. The bowl gave me a lot of trouble. I couldn't use my hat because of my skull. As for holding out my hand, that was quite out of the question. So I got a tin and hung it from a button of my greatcoat, what's the matter with me, of my coat, at pubis level. It did not hang plumb, it leaned respectfully towards the passer-by, he had only to drop his mite. But that obliged him to come up close to me, he was in danger of touching me. In the end I got a bigger tin, a kind of big tin box, and I placed it on the sidewalk at my feet. But people who give alms don't much care to toss them, there's something contemptuous about this gesture which is repugnant to sensitive natures. To say nothing of their having to aim. They are prepared to give, but not for their gift to go rolling under the passing feet or under the passing wheels, to be picked up perhaps by some undeserving person. So they don't give. There are those, to be sure, who stoop, but generally speaking people who give alms don't much care to stoop. What they like above all is to sight the wretch from afar, get ready their penny, drop it in their stride and hear the God bless you dying away in the distance. Personally I never said that, nor anything like it, I wasn't much of a believer, but I did make a noise with my mouth. In the end I got a kind of board or tray and tied it to my neck and waist. It jutted out just at the right height, pocket height, and its edge was far enough from my person for the coin to be bestowed without danger. Some days I strewed it with flowers, petals, buds and that herb which men call fleabane, I believe, in a word whatever I could find. I didn't go out of my way to look for them, but all the pretty things of this description that came my way were for the board. They must have thought I loved nature. Most of the time I looked up at the sky, but without focusing it, for why focus it? Most of the time it was a mixture of white, blue and grey, and then at evening all the evening colours. I felt it weighing softly on my face, I rubbed my face against it, one cheek after the other, turning my head from side to side. Now and then to rest my neck I dropped my head on my chest. Then I could see the board in the distance, a haze of many colours. I leaned against the wall, but without nonchalance, I shifted my weight from one foot to the other and my hands clutched the lapels of my coat. To beg with your hands in your pockets makes a bad impression, it irritates the workers, especially in winter. You should never wear gloves either. There were guttersnipes who swept away all I had earned, under cover of giving me a coin. It was to buy sweets. I unbuttoned my trousers discreetly to scratch myself. I scratched myself in an upward direction, with four nails. I pulled on the hairs, to get relief. It passed the time, time flew when I scratched myself. Real scratching is superior to masturbation, in my opinion. One can masturbate up to the age of seventy, and even beyond, but in the end it becomes a mere habit. Whereas to scratch myself properly I would have needed a dozen hands. I itched all over, on the privates, in the bush up to the navel, under the arms, in the arse, and then patches of eczema and psoriasis that I could set raging merely by thinking of them. It was in the arse I had the most pleasure, I stuck in my forefinger up to the knuckle. Later, if I had to shit, the pain was atrocious. But I hardly shat any more. Now and then a flying machine flew by, sluggishly it seemed to me. Often at the end of the day I discovered the legs of my trousers all wet. That must have been the dogs. I personally pissed very little. If by chance the need came on me a little squirt in my fly was enough to relieve it. Once at my post I did not leave it till nightfall. I had no appetite, God tempered the wind to me. After work I bought a bottle of milk and drank it in the evening in the shed. Better still, I got a little boy to buy it for me, always the same, they wouldn't serve me, I don't know why. I gave him a penny for his pains. One day I witnessed a strange scene. Normally I didn't see a great deal. I didn't hear a great deal either. I didn't pay attention. Strictly speaking I wasn't there. Strictly speaking I believe I've never been anywhere. But that day I must have come back. For some time past a sound had been scarifying me. I did not investigate the cause, for I said to myself, It's going to stop. But as it did not stop I had no choice but to find out the cause. It was a man perched on the roof of a car and haranguing the passers-by.

That at least was my interpretation. He was bellowing so loud that snatches of his discourse reached my ears. Union ... brothers ... Marx ... capital ... bread and butter ... love. It was all Greek to me. The car was drawn up against the kerb, just in front of me, I saw the orator from behind. All of a sudden he turned and pointed at me, as at an exhibit. Look at this down and out, he vociferated, this leftover. If he doesn't go down on all fours, it's for fear of being impounded. Old, lousy, rotten, ripe for the muckheap. And there are a thousand like him, worse than him, ten thousand, twenty thousand –. A voice, Thirty thousand. Every day you pass them by, resumed the orator, and when you have backed a winner you fling them a farthing. Do you ever think? The voice, God forbid. A penny, resumed the orator, tuppence –. The voice, Thruppence. It never enters your head, resumed the orator, that your charity is a crime, an incentive to slavery, stultification and organized murder. Take a good look at this living corpse. You may say it's his own fault. Ask him if it's his own fault. The voice, Ask him yourself. Then he bent forward and took me to task. I had perfected my board. It now consisted of two boards hinged together, which enabled me, when my work was done, to fold it and carry it under my arm. I liked doing little odd jobs. So I took off the rag, pocketed the few coins I had earned, untied the board, folded it and put it under my arm. Do you hear me, you crucified bastard! cried the orator. Then I went away, although it was still light. But generally speaking it was a quiet corner, busy but not overcrowded, thriving and well-frequented. He must have been a religious fanatic, I could find no other explanation. Perhaps he was an escaped lunatic. He had a nice face, a little on the red side.

I did not work every day. I had practically no expenses. I even managed to put a little aside, for my very last days. The days I did not work I spent lying in the shed. The shed was on a private estate, or what had once been a private estate, on the riverside. This estate, the main entrance to which opened on a narrow, dark and silent street, was enclosed with a wall, except of course on the river front, which marked its northern boundary for a distance of about thirty yards. From the last quays beyond the water the eyes rose to a confusion of low houses, wasteland, hoardings, chimneys, steeples and towers. A kind of parade ground was also to be seen, where soldiers played football all the year round. Only the ground-floor windows – no, I can't. The estate seemed abandoned. The gates were locked and the paths overgrown with grass. Only the ground-floor windows had shutters. The others were sometimes lit at night, faintly, now one, now another. At least that was my impression. Perhaps it was reflected light. In this shed, the day I adopted it, I found a boat, upside down. I righted it, chocked it up with stones and pieces of wood, took out the thwarts and made my bed inside. The rats had difficulty in getting at me, because of the bulge of the hull. And yet they longed to. Just think of it, living flesh, for in spite of everything I was still living flesh. I had lived too long among rats, in my chance dwellings, to share the dread they inspire in the vulgar. I even had a soft spot in my heart for them. They came with such confidence towards me, it seemed without the least repugnance. They made their toilet with catlike gestures. Toads at evening, motionless for hours, lap flies from the air. They like to squat where cover ends and open air begins, they favour thresholds. But I had to contend now with water rats, exceptionally lean and ferocious. So I made a kind of lid with stray boards. It's incredible the number of boards I've come across in my lifetime, I never needed a board but there it was, I had only to stoop and pick it up. I liked doing little odd jobs, no, not particularly, I didn't mind. It completely covered the boat, I'm referring again to the lid. I pushed it a little towards the stern, climbed into the boat by the bow, crawled to the stern, raised my feet and pushed the lid back towards the bow till it covered me completely. But what did my feet push against? They pushed against a cross-bar I nailed to the lid for that purpose, I liked these little odd jobs. But it was better to climb into the boat by the stern and pull back the lid with my hands till it completely covered me, then push it forward in the same way when I wanted to get out. As holds for my hands I planted two spikes just where I needed them. These little odds and ends of carpentry, if I may so describe it, carried out with whatever tools and material I chanced to find, gave me a certain pleasure. I knew it would soon be the end, so I played the part, you know, the part of – how shall I say, I don't know. I was comfortable enough in this boat, I must say. The lid fitted so well I had to pierce a hole. It's no good closing your eyes, you must leave them open in the dark, that is my opinion. I am not speaking of sleep, I am speaking of what I believe is called waking. In any case, I slept very little at this period, I wasn't sleepy, or I was too sleepy, I don't know, or I was afraid, I don't know. Flat then on my back I saw nothing except, dimly, just above my head, through the tiny chinks, the grey light of the shed. To see nothing at all, no, that's too much. I heard faintly the cries of the gulls ravening about the mouth of the sewer near by. In a spew of yellow foam, if my memory serves me right, the filth gushed into the river and the slush of birds above screaming with hunger and fury. I heard the lapping of water against the slip and against the bank and the other sound, so different, of open wave, I heard it too. I too, when I moved, felt less boat than wave, or so it seemed to me, and my stillness was the stillness of eddies. That may seem impossible. The rain too, I often heard it, for it often rained. Sometimes a drop, falling through the roof of the shed, exploded on me. All that composed a rather liquid world. And then of course there was the voice of the wind or rather those, so various, of its playthings. But what does it amount to? Howling, soughing, moaning, sighing. What I would have liked was hammer strokes, bang bang bang, clanging in the desert. I let farts to be sure, but hardly ever a real crack, they oozed out with a sucking noise, melted in the mighty never. I don't know how long I stayed there. I was very snug in my box, I must say. It seemed to me I had grown more independent of recent years. That no one came any more, that no one could come any more to ask me if I was all right and needed nothing, distressed me then but little. I was all right, yes, quite so, and the fear of getting worse was less with me. As for my needs, they had dwindled as it were to my dimensions and become, if I may say so, of so exquisite a quality as to exclude all thought of succour. To know I had a being, however faint and false, outside of me, had once had the power to stir my heart. You become unsociable, it's inevitable. It's enough to make you wonder sometimes if you are on the right planet. Even the words desert you, it's as bad as that. Perhaps it's the moment when the vessels stop communicating, you know, the vessels. There you are still between the two murmurs, it must be the same old song as ever, but Christ you wouldn't think so. There were times when I wanted to push away the lid and get out of the boat and couldn't, I was so indolent and weak, so content deep down where I was. I felt them hard upon me, the icy, tumultuous streets, the terrifying faces, the noises that slash, pierce, claw, bruise. So I waited till the desire to shit, or even to piss, lent me wings. I did not want to dirty my nest! And yet it sometimes happened, and even more and more often. Arched and rigid I edged down my trousers and turned a little on my side, just enough to free the hole. To contrive a little kingdom, in the midst of the universal muck, then shit on it, ah that was me all over. The excrements were me too, I know, I know, but all the same. Enough, enough, the next thing I was having visions, I who never did, except sometimes in my sleep, who never had, real visions, I'd remember, except perhaps as a child, my myth will have it so. I knew they were visions because it was night and I was alone in my boat. What else could they have been? So I was in my boat and gliding on the waters. I didn't have to row, the ebb was carrying me out. Anyway I saw no oars, they must have taken them away. I had a board, the remains of a thwart perhaps, which I used when I came too close to the bank, or when a pier came bearing down on me or a barge at its moorings. There were stars in the sky, quite a few. I didn't know what the weather was doing, I was neither cold nor warm and all seemed calm. The banks receded more and more, it was inevitable, soon I saw them no more. The lights grew fainter and fewer as the river widened. There on the land men were sleeping, bodies were gathering strength for the toil and joys of the morrow. The boat was not gliding now, it was tossing, buffeted by the choppy waters of the bay. All seemed calm and yet foam was washing aboard. Now the sea air was all about me, I had no other shelter than the land, and what does it amount to, the shelter of the land, at such a time. I saw the beacons, four in all, including a lightship. I knew them well, even as a child I had known them well. It was evening, I was with my father on a height, he held my hand. I would have liked him to draw me close with a gesture of protective love, but his mind was on other things. He also taught me the names of the mountains. But to have done with these visions I also saw the lights of the buoys, the sea seemed full of them, red and green, and to my surprise even yellow. And on the slopes of the mountain, now rearing its unbroken bulk behind the town, the fires turned from gold to red, from red to gold. I knew what it was, it was the gorse burning. How often I had set a match to it myself, as a child. And hours later, back in my home, before I climbed into bed, I watched from my high window the fires I had lit. That night then, all aglow with distant fires, on sea, on land and in the sky, I drifted with the currents and the tides. I noticed that my hat was tied, with a string I suppose, to my buttonhole. I got up from my seat in the stern and a great clanking was heard. That was the chain. One end was fastened to the bow and the other round my waist. I must have pierced a hole beforehand in the floor-boards, for there I was down on my knees prying out the plug with my knife. The hole was small and the water rose slowly. It would take a good half hour, everything included, barring accidents. Back now in the stern-sheets, my legs stretched out, my back well propped against the sack stuffed with grass I used as a cushion, I swallowed my calmative. The sea, the sky, the mountains and the islands closed in and crushed me in a mighty systole, then scattered to the uttermost confines of space. The memory came faint and cold of the story I might have told, a story in the likeness of my life, I mean without the courage to end or the strength to go on.

Translated by Richard Seaver
in collaboration with the author

The Expelled

There were not many steps. I had counted them a thousand times, both going up and coming down, but the figure has gone from my mind. I have never known whether you should say one with your foot on the sidewalk, two with the following foot on the first step, and so on, or whether the sidewalk shouldn't count. At the top of the steps I fell foul of the same dilemma. In the other direction, I mean from top to bottom, it was the same, the word is not too strong. I did not know where to begin nor where to end, that's the truth of the matter. I arrived therefore at three totally different figures, without ever knowing which of them was right. And when I say that the figure has gone from my mind, I mean that none of the three figures is with me any more, in my mind. It is true that if I were to find, in my mind, where it is certainly to be found, one of these figures, I would find it and it alone, without being able to deduce from it the other two. And even were I to recover two, I would not know the third. No, I would have to find all three, in my mind, in order to know all three. Memories are killing. So you must not think of certain things, of those that are dear to you, or rather you must think of them, for if you don't there is the danger of finding them, in your mind, little by little. That is to say, you must think of them for a while, a good while, every day several times a day, until they sink forever in the mud. That's an order.

After all it is not the number of steps that matters. The important thing to remember is that there were not many, and that I have remembered. Even for the child there were not many, compared to other steps he knew, from seeing them every day, from going up them and coming down, and from playing on them at knuckle-bones and other games the very names of which he has forgotten. What must it have been like then for the man I had overgrown into?

The fall was therefore not serious. Even as I fell I heard the door slam, which brought me a little comfort, in the midst of my fall. For that meant they were not pursuing me down into the street, with a stick, to beat me in full view of the passers-by. For if that had been their intention they would not have shut the door, but left it open, so that the persons assembled in the vestibule might enjoy my chastisement and be edified. So, for once, they had confined themselves to throwing me out and no more about it. I had time, before coming to rest in the gutter, to conclude this piece of reasoning.

Under these circumstances nothing compelled me to get up immediately. I rested my elbow on the sidewalk, funny the things you remember, settled my ear in the cup of my hand and began to reflect on my situation, notwithstanding its familiarity. But the sound, fainter but unmistakable, of the door slammed again, roused me from my reverie, in which already a whole landscape was taking form, charming with hawthorn and wild roses, most dreamlike, and made me look up in alarm, my hands flat on the sidewalk and my legs braced for flight. But it was merely my hat sailing towards me through the air, rotating as it came. I caught it and put it on. They were most correct, according to their god. They could have kept this hat, but it was not theirs, it was mine, so they gave it back to me. But the spell was broken.

How describe this hat? And why? When my head had

attained I shall not say its definitive but its maximum dimensions, my father said to me, Come, son, we are going to buy your hat, as though it had pre-existed from time immemorial in a pre-established place. He went straight to the hat. I personally had no say in the matter, nor had the hatter. I have often wondered if my father's purpose was not to humiliate me, if he was not jealous of me who was young and handsome, fresh at least, while he was already old and all bloated and purple. It was forbidden me, from that day forth, to go out bareheaded, my pretty brown hair blowing in the wind. Sometimes, in a secluded street, I took it off and held it in my hand, but trembling. I was required to brush it morning and evening. Boys my age with whom, in spite of everything, I was obliged to mix occasionally, mocked me. But I said to myself, It is not really the hat, they simply make merry at the hat because it is a little more glaring than the rest, for they have no finesse. I have always been amazed at my contemporaries' lack of finesse, I whose soul writhed from morning to night, in the mere quest of itself. But perhaps they were simply being kind, like those who make game of the hunchback's big nose. When my father died I could have got rid of this hat, there was nothing more to prevent me, but not I. But how describe it? Some other time, some other time.

I got up and set off. I forget how old I can have been. In what had just happened to me there was nothing in the least memorable. It was neither the cradle nor the grave of anything whatever. Or rather it resembled so many other cradles, so many other graves, that I'm lost. But I don't believe I exaggerate when I say that I was in the prime of life, what I believe is called the full possession of one's faculties. Ah yes, them I possessed all right. I crossed the street and turned back towards the house that had just ejected me, I who never turned back when leaving. How beautiful it was! There were geraniums in the windows. I have brooded over geraniums for years. Geraniums are artful customers, but in the end I was able to do what I liked with them. I have always greatly admired the door of this house, up on top of its little flight of steps. How describe it? It was a massive green door, encased in summer in a kind of green and white striped housing, with a hole for the thunderous wrought-iron knocker and a slit for letters, this latter closed to dust, flies and tits by a brass flap fitted with springs. So much for that description. The door was set between two pillars of the same colour, the bell being on that to the right. The curtains were in unexceptionable taste. Even the smoke rising from one of the chimney-pots seemed to spread and vanish in the air more sorrowful than the neighbours', and bluer. I looked up at the third and last floor and saw my window outrageously open. A thorough cleansing was in full swing. In a few hours they would close the window, draw the curtains and spray the whole place with disinfectant. I knew them. I would have gladly died in that house. In a sort of vision I saw the door open and my feet come out.

I wasn't afraid to look, for I knew they were not spying on me from behind the curtains, as they could have done if they had wished. But I knew them. They had all gone back into their dens and resumed their occupations.

And yet I had done them no harm.

I did not know the town very well, scene of my birth and of my first steps in this world, and then of all the others, so many that I thought all trace of me was lost, but I was wrong. I went out so little! Now and then I would go to the window, part the curtains and look out. But then I hastened back to the depths of the room, where the bed was. I felt ill at ease with all this air about me, lost before the confusion of innumerable prospects. But I still knew how to act at this period, when it was absolutely necessary. But first I raised my eyes to the sky, whence cometh our help, where there are no roads, where you wander freely, as in a desert, and where nothing obstructs your vision, wherever you turn your eyes, but the limits of vision itself. When I was younger I thought life would be good in the middle of a plain and went to the Lüneburg heath. With the plain in my head I went to the heath. There were other heaths far less remote, but a voice kept saying to me, It's the Lüneburg heath you need. The element lüne must have had something to do with it. As it turned out the Lüneburg heath was most unsatisfactory, most unsatisfactory. I came home disappointed, and at the same time relieved. Yes, I don't know why, but I have never been disappointed, and I often was in the early days, without feeling at the same time, or a moment later, an undeniable relief.

I set off. What a gait. Stiffness of the lower limbs, as if nature had denied me knees, extraordinary splaying of the feet to right and left of the line of march. The trunk, on the contrary, as if by the effect of a compensatory mechanism, was as flabby as an old ragbag, tossing wildly to the unpredictable jolts of the pelvis. I have often tried to correct these defects, to stiffen my bust, flex my knees and walk with my feet in front of one another, for I had at least five or six, but it always ended in the same way, I mean with a loss of equilibrium, followed by a fall. A man must walk without paying attention to what he's doing, as he sighs, and when I walked without paying attention to what I was doing I walked in the way I have just described, and when I began to pay attention I managed a few steps of creditable execution and then fell. I decided therefore to be myself. This carriage is due, in my opinion, in part at least, to a certain leaning from which I have never been able to free myself completely and which left its stamp, as was only to be expected, on my impressionable years, those which govern the fabrication of character, I refer to the period which extends, as far as the eye can see, from the first totterings, behind a chair, to the third form, in which I concluded my studies. I had then the deplorable habit, having pissed in my trousers, or shat there, which I did fairly regularly early in the morning, about ten or half past ten, of persisting in going on and finishing my day as if nothing had happened. The very idea of changing my trousers, or of confiding in mother, who goodness knows asked nothing better than to help me, was unbearable, I don't know why, and till bedtime I dragged on with burning and stinking between my little thighs, or sticking to my bottom, the result of my incontinence. Whence this wary way of walking, with the legs stiff and wide apart, and this desperate rolling of the bust, no doubt intended to put people off the scent, to make them think I was full of gaiety and high spirits, without a care in the world, and to lend plausibility to my explanations concerning my nether rigidity, which I ascribed to hereditary rheumatism. My youthful ardour, in so far as I had any, spent itself in this effort, I became sour and mistrustful, a little before my time, in love with hiding and the prone position. Poor juvenile solutions, explaining nothing. No need then for caution, we may reason on to our heart's content, the fog won't lift.

The weather was fine. I advanced down the street, keeping as close as I could to the sidewalk. The widest sidewalk is never wide enough for me, once I set myself in motion, and I hate to inconvenience strangers. A policeman stopped me and said, The street for vehicles, the sidewalk for pedestrians. Like a bit of Old Testament. So I got back on the sidewalk, almost apologetically, and persevered there, in spite of an indescribable jostle, for a good twenty steps, till I had to fling myself to the ground to avoid crushing a child. He was wearing a little harness, I remember, with little bells, he must have taken himself for a pony, or a Clydesdale, why not. I would have crushed him gladly, I loathe children, and it would have been doing him a service, but I was afraid of reprisals. Everyone is a parent, that is what keeps you from hoping. One should reserve, on busy streets, special tracks for these nasty little creatures, their prams, hoops, sweets, scooters, skates, grandpas, grandmas, nannies, balloons and balls, all their foul little happiness in a word. I fell then, and brought down with me an old lady covered with spangles and lace, who must have weighed about sixteen stone. Her screams soon drew a crowd. I had high hopes she had broken her femur, old ladies break their femur easily, but not enough, not enough. I took advantage of the confusion to make off, muttering unintelligible oaths, as if I were the victim, and I was, but I couldn't have proved it. They never lynch children, babies, no matter what they do they are whitewashed in advance. I personally would lynch them with the utmost pleasure, I don't say I'd lend a hand, no, I am not a violent man, but I'd encourage the others and stand them drinks when it was done. But no sooner had I begun to reel on than I was stopped by a second policeman, similar in all respects to the first, so much so that I wondered whether it was not the same one. He pointed out to me that the sidewalk was for everyone, as if it was quite obvious that I could not be assimilated to that category. Would you like me, I said, without thinking for a single moment of Heraclitus, to get down in the gutter? Get down wherever you want, he said, but leave some room for others. If you can't bloody well get about like everyone else, he said, you'd do better to stay at home. It was exactly my feeling. And that he should attribute to me a home was no small satisfaction. At that moment a funeral passed, as sometimes happens. There was a great flurry of hats and at the same time a flutter of countless fingers. Personally if I were reduced to making the sign of the cross I would set my heart on doing it right, nose, navel, left nipple, right nipple. But the way they did it, slovenly and wild, he seemed crucified all of a heap, no dignity, his knees under his chin and his hands anyhow. The more fervent stopped dead and muttered. As for the policeman he stiffened to attention, closed his eyes and saluted. Through the windows of the cabs I caught a glimpse of the mourners conversing with animation, no doubt scenes from the life of their late dear brother in Christ, or sister. I seem to have heard that the hearse trappings are not the same in both cases, but I never could find out what the difference consists in. The horses were farting and shitting as if they were going to the fair. I saw no one kneeling.

But with us the last journey is soon done, it is in vain you quicken your pace, the last cab containing the domestics soon leaves you behind, the respite is over, the bystanders go their ways, you may look to yourself again. So I stopped a third time, of my own free will, and entered a cab. Those I had just seen pass, crammed with people hotly arguing, must have made a strong impression on me. It's a big black box, rocking and swaying on its springs, the windows are small, you curl up in a corner, it smells musty. I felt my hat grazing the roof. A little later I leant forward and closed the windows. Then I sat down again with my back to the horse. I was dozing off when a voice made me start, the cabman's. He had opened the door, no doubt despairing of making himself heard through the window. All I saw was his moustache. Where to? he said. He had climbed down from his seat on purpose to ask me that. And I who thought I was far away already. I reflected, searching in my memory for the name of a street, or a monument. Is your cab for sale? I said. I added, Without the horse. What would I do with a horse? But what would I do with a cab? Could I as much as stretch out in it? Who would bring me food? To the Zoo, I said. It is rare for a capital to be without a Zoo. I added, Don't go too fast. He laughed. The suggestion that he might go too fast to the Zoo must have amused him. Unless it was the prospect of being cabless. Unless it was simply myself, my own person, whose presence in the cab must have transformed it, so much so that the cabman, seeing me there with my head in the shadows of the roof and my knees against the window, had wondered perhaps if it was really his cab, really a cab. He hastens to look at his horse, and is reassured. But does one ever know oneself why one laughs? His laugh in any case was brief, which suggested I was not the joke. He closed the door and climbed back to his seat. It was not long then before the horse got under way.

Yes, surprising though it may seem, I still had a little money at this time. The small sum my father had left me as a gift, with no restrictions, at his death, I still wonder if it wasn't stolen from me. Then I had none. And yet my life went on, and even in the way I wanted, up to a point. The great disadvantage of this condition, which might be defined as the absolute impossibility of all purchase, is that it compels you to bestir yourself. It is rare, for example, when you are completely penniless, that you can have food brought to you from time to time in your retreat. You are therefore obliged to go out and bestir yourself, at least one day a week. You can hardly have a home address under these circumstances, it's inevitable. It was therefore with a certain delay that I learnt they were looking for me, for an affair concerning me. I forget through what channel. I did not read the newspapers, nor do I remember having spoken with anyone during these years, except perhaps three or four times, on the subject of food. At any rate, I must have had wind of the affair one way or another, otherwise I would never have gone to see the lawyer, Mr Nidder, strange how one fails to forget certain names, and he would never have received me. He verified my identity. That took some time. I showed him the metal initials in the lining of my hat, they proved nothing but they increased the probabilities. Sign, he said. He played with a cylindrical ruler, you could have felled an ox with it. Count, he said. A young woman, perhaps venal, was present at this interview, as a witness no doubt. I stuffed the wad in my pocket. You shouldn't do that, he said. It occurred to me that he should have asked me to count before I signed, it would have been more in order. Where can I reach you, he said, if necessary? At the foot of the stairs I thought of something. Soon after I went back to ask him where this money came from, adding that I had a right to know. He gave me a woman's name that I've forgotten. Perhaps she had dandled me on her knees while I was still in swaddling clothes and there had been some lovey-dovey. Sometimes that suffices. I repeat, in swaddling clothes, for any later it would have been too late, for lovey-dovey. It is thanks to this money then that I still had a little. Very little. Divided by my life to come it was negligible, unless my conjectures were unduly pessimistic. I knocked on the partition beside my hat, right in the cabman's back if my calculations were correct. A cloud of dust rose from the upholstery. I took a stone from my pocket and knocked with the stone, until the cab stopped. I noticed that, unlike most vehicles, which slow down before stopping, the cab stopped dead. I waited. The whole cab shook. The cabman, on his high seat, must have been listening. I saw the horse as with my eyes of flesh. It had not lapsed into the drooping attitude of its briefest halts, it remained alert, its ears pricked up. I looked out of the window, we were again in motion. I banged again on the partition, until the cab stopped again. The cabman got down cursing from his seat. I lowered the window to prevent his opening the door. Faster, faster. He was redder than ever, purple in other words. Anger, or the rushing wind. I told him I was hiring him for the day. He replied that he had a funeral at three o'clock. Ah the dead. I told him I had changed my mind and no longer wished to go to the Zoo. Let us not go to the Zoo, I said. He replied that it made no difference to him where we went, provided it wasn't too far, because of his beast. And they talk to us about the specificity of primitive peoples' speech. I asked him if he knew of an eating-house. I added, You'll eat with me. I prefer being with a regular customer in such places. There was a long table with two benches of exactly the same length on either side. Across the table he spoke to me of his life, of his wife, of his beast, then again of his life, of the atrocious life that was his, chiefly because of his character. He asked me if I realized what it meant to be out of doors in all weathers. I learnt there were still some cabmen who spent their day snug and warm inside their cabs on the rank, waiting for a customer to come and rouse them. Such a thing was possible in the past, but nowadays other methods were necessary, if a man was to have a little laid up at the end of his days. I described my situation to him, what I had lost and what I was looking for. We did our best, both of us, to understand, to explain. He understood that I had lost my room and needed another, but all the rest escaped him. He had taken it into his head, whence nothing could ever dislodge it, that I was looking for a furnished room. He took from his pocket an evening paper of the day before, or perhaps the day before that again, and proceeded to run through the advertisements, five or six of which he underlined with a tiny pencil, the same that hovered over the likely outsiders. He underlined no doubt those he would have underlined if he had been in my shoes, or perhaps those concentrated in the same area, because of his beast. I would only have confused him by saying that I could tolerate no furniture in my room except the bed, and that all the other pieces, and even the very night-table, had to be removed before I would consent to set foot in it. About three o'clock we roused the horse and set off again. The cabman suggested I climb up beside him on the seat, but for some time already I had been dreaming of the inside of the cab and I got back inside. We visited, methodically I hope, one after another, the addresses he had underlined. The short winter's day was drawing to a close. It seems to me sometimes that these are the only days I have ever known, and especially that most charming moment of all, just before night wipes them out. The addresses he had underlined, or rather marked with a cross, as common people do, proved fruitless one by one, and one by one he crossed them out with a diagonal stroke. Later he showed me the paper, advising me to keep it safe so as to be sure not to look again where I had already looked in vain. In spite of the closed windows, the creaking of the cab and the traffic noises, I heard him singing, all alone aloft on his seat. He had preferred me to a funeral, this was a fact which would endure forever. He sang, *She is far from the land where her young hero*, those are the only words I remember. At each stop he got down from his seat and helped me down from mine. I rang at the door he directed me to and sometimes I disappeared inside the house. It was a strange feeling, I remember, a house all about me again, after so long. He waited for me on the sidewalk and helped me climb back into the cab. I was sick and tired of this cabman. He clambered back to his seat and we set off again. At a certain moment there occurred this. He stopped. I shook off my torpor and made ready to get down. But he did not come to open the door and offer me his arm, so that I was obliged to get down by myself. He was lighting the lamps. I love oil lamps, in spite of their having been, with candles, and if I except the stars, the first lights I ever knew. I asked him if I might light the second lamp, since he had already lit the first himself. He gave me his box of matches, I swung open on its hinges the little convex glass, lit and closed at once, so that the wick might burn steady and bright, snug in its little house, sheltered from the wind. I had this joy. We saw nothing, by the light of these lamps, save the vague outlines of the horse, but the others saw them from afar, two yellow glows sailing slowly through the air. When the equipage turned an eye could be seen, red or green as the case might be, a bossy rhomb as clear and keen as stained glass.

After we had verified the last address the cabman suggested bringing me to a hotel he knew where I would be comfortable. That makes sense, cabman, hotel, it's plausible. With his recommendation I would want for nothing. Every convenience, he said, with a wink. I place this conversation on the sidewalk, in front of the house from which I had just emerged. I remember, beneath the lamp, the flank of the horse, hollow and damp, and on the handle of the door the cabman's hand in its woollen glove. The roof of the cab was on a level with my neck. I suggested we have a drink. The horse had neither eaten nor drunk all day. I mentioned this to the cabman, who replied that his beast would take no food till it was back in the stable. If it ate anything whatever, during work, were it but an apple or a lump of sugar, it would have stomach pains and colics that would root it to the spot and might even kill it. That was why he was compelled to tie its jaws together with a strap whenever for one reason or another he had to let it out of his sight, so that it would not have to suffer from the kind hearts of the passers-by. After a few drinks the cabman invited me to do his wife and him the honour of spending the night in their home. It was not far. Recollecting these emotions, with the celebrated advantage of tranquillity, it seems to me he did nothing else, all that day, but turn about his lodging. They lived above a stable, at the back of a yard. Ideal location, I could have done with it. Having presented me to his wife, extraordinarily full-bottomed, he left us. She was manifestly ill at ease, alone with me. I could understand her, I don't stand on ceremony on these occasions. No reason for this to end or go on. Then let it end. I said I would go down to the stable and sleep there. The cabman protested. I insisted. He drew his wife's attention to the pustule on top of my skull, for I had removed my hat out of civility. He should have that removed, she said. The cabman named a doctor he held in high esteem who had rid him of an induration of the seat. If he wants to sleep in the stable, said his wife, let him sleep in the stable. The cabman took the lamp from the table and preceded me down the stairs, or rather ladder, which descended to the stable, leaving his wife in the dark. He spread a horse blanket on the ground in a corner on the straw and left me a box of matches in case I needed to see clearly in the night. I don't remember what the horse was doing all this time. Stretched out in the dark I heard the noise it made as it drank, a noise like no other, the sudden gallop of the rats and above me the muffled voices of the cabman and his wife as they criticized me. I held the box of matches in my hand, a big box of safety matches. I got up during the night and struck one. Its brief flame enabled me to locate the cab. I was seized, then abandoned, by the desire to set fire to the stable. I found the cab in the dark, opened the door, the rats poured out, I climbed in. As I settled down I noticed that the cab was no longer level, it was inevitable, with the shafts resting on the ground. It was better so, that allowed me to lie well back, with my feet higher than my head on the other seat. Several times during the night I felt the horse looking at me through the window and the breath of its nostrils. Now that it was unharnessed it must have been puzzled by my presence in the cab. I was cold, having forgotten to take the blanket, but not quite enough to go and get it. Through the window of the cab I saw the window of the stable, more and more clearly. I got out of the cab. It was not so dark now in the stable, I could make out the manger, the rack, the harness hanging, what else, buckets and brushes. I went to the door but couldn't open it. The horse didn't take its eyes off me. Don't horses ever sleep? It seemed to me the cabman should have tied it, to the manger for example. So I was obliged to leave by the window. It wasn't easy. But what is easy? I went out head first, my hands were flat on the ground of the yard while my legs were still thrashing to get clear of the frame. I remember the tufts of grass on which I pulled with both hands, in my effort to extricate myself. I should have taken off my greatcoat and thrown it through the window, but that would have meant thinking of it. No sooner had I left the yard than I thought of something. Weakness. I slipped a banknote in the matchbox, went back to the yard and placed the box on the sill of the window through which I had just come. The horse was at the window. But after I had taken a few steps in the street I returned to the yard and took back my banknote. I left the matches, they were not mine. The horse was still at the window. I was sick and tired of this cabhorse. Dawn was just breaking. I did not know where I was. I made towards the rising sun, towards where I thought it should rise, the quicker to come into the light. I would have liked a sea horizon, or a desert one. When I am abroad in the morning I go to meet the sun, and in the evening, when I am abroad, I follow it, till I am down among the dead. I don't know why I told this story. I could just as well have told another. Perhaps some other time I'll be able to tell another. Living souls, you will see how alike they are.

Translated by Richard Seaver
in collaboration with the author

The Calmative

I don't know when I died. It always seemed to me I died old, about ninety years old, and what years, and that my body bore it out, from head to foot. But this evening, alone in my icy bed, I have the feeling I'll be older than the day, the night, when the sky with all its lights fell upon me, the same I had so often gazed on since my first stumblings on the distant earth. For I'm too frightened this evening to listen to myself rot, waiting for the great red lapses of the heart, the tearings at the caecal walls, and for the slow killings to finish in my skull, the assaults on unshakable pillars, the fornications with corpses. So I'll tell myself a story, I'll try and tell myself another story, to try and calm myself, and it's there I feel I'll be old, old, even older than the day I fell, calling for help, and it came. Or is it possible that in this story I have come back to life, after my death? No, it's not like me to come back to life, after my death.

What possessed me to stir when I wasn't with anybody? Was I being thrown out? No, I wasn't with anybody. I see a kind of den littered with empty tins. And yet we are not in the country. Perhaps it's just ruins, a ruined folly, on the skirts of the town, in a field, for the fields come right up to our walls, their walls, and the cows lie down at night in the lee of the ramparts. I have changed refuge so often, in the course of my rout, that now I can't tell between dens and ruins. But there was never any city but the one. It is true you often move along in a dream, houses and factories darken the air, trams go by and under your feet wet from the grass there are suddenly cobbles. I only know the city of my childhood, I must have seen the other, but unbelieving. All I say cancels out, I'll have said nothing. Was I hungry itself? Did the weather tempt me? It was cloudy and cool, I insist, but not to the extent of luring me out. I couldn't get up at the first attempt, nor let us say at the second, and once up, propped against the wall, I wondered if I could go on, I mean up, propped against the wall. Impossible to go out and walk. I speak as though it all happened yesterday. Yesterday indeed is recent, but not enough. For what I tell this evening is passing this evening, at this passing hour. I'm no longer with these assassins, in this bed of terror, but in my distant refuge, my hands twined together, my head bowed, weak, breathless, calm, free, and older than I'll have ever been, if my calculations are correct. I'll tell my story in the past none the less, as though it were a myth, or an old fable, for this evening I need another age, that age to become another age in which I became what I was.

But little by little I got myself out and started walking with short steps among the trees, oh look, trees! The paths of other days were rank with tangled growth. I leaned against the trunks to get my breath and pulled myself forward with the help of boughs. Of my last passage no trace remained. They were the perishing oaks immortalized by d'Aubigné. It was only a grove. The fringe was near, a light less green and kind of tattered told me so, in a whisper. Yes, no matter where you stood, in this little wood, and were it in the furthest recess of its poor secrecies, you saw on every hand the gleam of this pale light, promise of God knows what fatuous eternity. Die without too much pain, a little, that's worth your while. Under the blind sky close with your own hands the eyes soon sockets, then quick into carrion not to mislead the crows. That's the advantage of death by drowning, one of the advantages, the crabs never get there too soon. But here a strange thing, I was no sooner free of the wood at last, having crossed unminding the ditch that girdles it, than thoughts came to me of cruelty, the kind that smiles. A lush pasture lay before me, nonsuch perhaps, who cares, drenched in evening dew or recent rain. Beyond this meadow to my certain knowledge a path, then a field and finally the ramparts, closing the prospect. Cyclopean and crenellated, standing out faintly against a sky scarcely less sombre, they did not seem in ruins, viewed from mine, but were, to my certain knowledge. Such was the scene offered to me, in vain, for I knew it well and loathed it. What I saw was a bald man in a brown suit, a comedian. He was telling a funny story about a fiasco. Its point escaped me. He used the word snail, or slug, to the delight of all present. The women seemed even more entertained than their escorts, if that were possible. Their shrill laughter pierced the clapping and, when this had subsided, broke out still here and there in sudden peals even after the next story had begun, so that part of it was lost. Perhaps they had in mind the reigning penis sitting who knows by their side and from that sweet shore launched their cries of joy towards the comic vast, what a talent. But it's to me this evening something has to happen, to my body as in myth and metamorphosis, this old body to which nothing ever happened, or so little, which never met with anything, loved anything, wished for anything, in its tarnished universe, except for the mirrors to shatter, the plane, the curved, the magnifying, the minifying, and to vanish in the havoc of its images. Yes, this evening it has to be as in the story my father used to read to me, evening after evening, when I was small, and he had all his health, to calm me, evening after evening, year after year it seems to me this evening, which I don't remember much about, except that it was the adventures of one Joe Breem, or Breen, the son of a lighthouse-keeper, a strong muscular lad of fifteen, those were the words, who swam for miles in the night, a knife between his teeth, after a shark, I forget why, out of sheer heroism. He might have simply told me the story, he knew it by heart, so did I, but that wouldn't have calmed me, he had to read it to me, evening after evening, or pretend to read it to me, turning the pages and explaining the pictures that were of me already, evening after evening the same pictures till I dozed off on his shoulder. If he had skipped a single word I would have hit him, with my little fist, in his big belly bursting out of the old cardigan and unbuttoned trousers that rested him from his office canonicals. For me now the setting forth, the struggle and perhaps the return, for the old man I am this evening, older than my father ever was, older than I shall ever be. I crossed the meadow with little stiff steps at the same time limp, the best I could manage. Of my last passage no trace remained, it was long ago. And the little bruised stems soon straighten up again, having need of air and light, and as for the broken their place is soon taken. I entered the town by what they call the Shepherds' Gate without having seen a soul, only the first bats like flying crucifixions, nor heard a sound except my steps, my heart in my breast and then, as I went under the arch, the hoot of an owl, that cry at once so soft and fierce which in the night, calling, answering, through my little wood and those nearby, sounded in my shelter like a tocsin. The further I went into the city the more I was struck by its deserted air. It was lit as usual, brighter than usual, although the shops were shut. But the lights were on in their windows with the object no doubt of attracting customers and prompting them to say, I say, I like that, not dear either, I'll come back tomorrow, if I'm still alive. I nearly said, Good God it's Sunday. The trams were running, the buses too, but few, slow, empty, noiseless, as if under water. I didn't see a single horse! I was wearing my long green greatcoat with the velvet collar, such as motorists wore about 1900, my father's, but that day it was sleeveless, a vast cloak. But on me it was still the same great dead weight, with no warmth to it, and the tails swept the ground, scraped it rather, they had grown so stiff, and I so shrunken. What would, what could happen to me in this empty place? But I felt the houses packed with people, lurking behind the curtains they looked out into the street or, crouched far back in the depths of the room, head in hands, were sunk in dream. Up aloft my hat, the same as always, I reached no further. I went right across the city and came to the sea, having followed the river to its mouth. I kept saying, I'll go back, unbelieving. The boats at anchor in the harbour, tied up to the jetty, seemed no less numerous than usual, as if I knew anything about what was usual. But the quays were deserted and there was no sign or stir of arrival or departure. But all might change from one moment to the next and be transformed like magic before my eyes. Then all the bustle of the people and things of the sea, the masts of the big craft gravely rocking and of the small more jauntily, I insist, and I'd hear the gulls' terrible cry and perhaps the sailors' cry. And I might slip unnoticed aboard a freighter outward bound and get far away and spend far away a few good months, perhaps even a year or two, in the sun, in peace, before I died. And without going that far it would be a sad state of affairs if in that unscandalizable throng I couldn't achieve a little encounter that would calm me a little, or exchange a few words with a navigator for example, words to carry away with me to my refuge, to add to my collection. I waited sitting on a kind of topless capstan, saying, The very capstans this evening are out of order. And I gazed out to sea, out beyond the breakwaters, without sighting the least vessel.

I could see lights flush with the water. And the pretty beacons at the harbour mouth I could see too, and others in the distance, flashing from the coast, the islands, the headlands. But seeing still no sign or stir I made ready to go, to turn away sadly from this dead haven, for there are scenes that call for strange farewells. I had merely to bow my head and look down at my feet, for it is in this attitude I always drew the strength to, how shall I say, I don't know, and it was always from the earth, rather than from the sky, notwithstanding its reputation, that my help came in time of trouble. And there, on the flagstone, which I was not focusing, for why focus it, I saw haven afar, where the black swell was most perilous, and all about me storm and wreck. I'll never come back here, I said. But when with a thrust of both hands against the the rim of the capstan I heaved myself up I found facing me a young boy holding a goat by a horn. I sat down again. He stood there silent looking at me without visible fear or revulsion. Admittedly the light was poor. His silence seemed natural to me, it befitted me as the elder to speak first. He was barefoot and in rags. Haunter of the waterfront he had stepped aside to see what the dark hulk could be abandoned on the quayside. Such was my train of thought. Close up to me now with his little guttersnipe's eye there could be no doubt left in his mind. And yet he stayed. Can this base thought be mine? Moved, for after all that is what I must have come out for, in a way, and with little expectation of advantage from what might follow, I resolved to speak to him. So I marshalled the words and opened my mouth, thinking I would hear them. But all I heard was a kind of rattle, unintelligible even to me who knew what was intended. But it was nothing, mere speechlessness due to long silence, as in the wood that darkens the mouth of hell, do you remember, I only just. Without letting go of his goat he moved right up against me and offered me a sweet out of a twist of paper such as you could buy for a penny. I hadn't been offered a sweet for eighty years at least, but I took it eagerly and put it in my mouth, the old gesture came back to me, more and more moved since that is what I wanted. The sweets were stuck together and I had my work cut out to separate the top one, a green one, from the others, but he helped me and his hand brushed mine. And a moment later as he made to move away, hauling his goat after him, with a great gesticulation of my whole body I motioned him to stay and I said, in an impetuous murmur, Where are you off to, my little man, with your nanny? The words were hardly out of my mouth when for shame I covered my face. And yet they were the same I had tried to utter but a moment before. Where are you off to, my little man, with your nanny! If I could have blushed I would have, but there was not enough blood left in my extremities. If I had had a penny in my pocket I would have given it to him, for him to forgive me, but I did not have a penny in my pocket, nor anything resembling it. Nothing that could give pleasure to a little unfortunate at the mouth of life. I suspect I had nothing with me but my stone, that day, having gone out as it were without premeditation. Of his little person I was fated to see no more than the black curly hair and the pretty curve of the long bare legs all muscle and dirt. And the hand, so fresh and keen, I would not forget in a hurry either. I looked for better words to say to him, I found them too late, he was gone, oh not far, but far. Out of my life too he went without a care, not one of his thoughts would ever be for me again, unless perhaps when he was old and, delving in his boyhood, would come upon that gallows night and hold the goat by the horn again and linger again a moment by my side, with who knows perhaps a touch of tenderness, even of envy, but I have my doubts. Poor dear dumb beasts, how you will have helped me. What does your daddy do? that's what

I would have said to him if he had given me the chance. Soon they were no more than a single blur which if I hadn't known I might have taken for a young centaur. I was nearly going to have the goat dung, then pick up a handful of the pellets so soon cold and hard, sniff and even taste them, no, that would not help me this evening. I say this evening as if it were always the same evening, but are there two evenings? I went, intending to get back as fast as I could, but it would not be quite empty-handed, repeating, I'll never come back here. My legs were paining me, every step would gladly have been the last, but the glances I darted towards the windows, stealthily, showed me a great cylinder sweeping past as though on rollers on the asphalt. I must indeed have been moving fast, for I overhauled more than one pedestrian, there are the first men, without extending myself, I who in the normal way was left standing by cripples, and then I seemed to hear the footfalls die behind me. And yet each little step would gladly have been the last. So much so that when I emerged on a square I hadn't noticed on the way out, with a cathedral looming on the far side, I decided to go in, if it was open, and hide, as in the Middle Ages, for a space. I say cathedral, it may not have been, I don't know, all I know is it would vex me in this story that aspires to be the last, to have taken refuge in a common church. I remarked the Saxon Stützenwechsel. Charming effect, but it didn't charm me. The brilliantly lit nave appeared deserted. I walked round it several times without seeing a soul. They were hiding perhaps, under the choir-stalls, or dodging behind the pillars, like woodpeckers. Suddenly close to where I was, and without my having heard the long preliminary rumblings, the organ began to boom. I sprang up from the mat on which I lay before the altar and hastened to the far end of the nave as if on my way out. But it was a side aisle and the door I disappeared through was not the exit. For instead of being restored to the night I found myself at the foot of a spiral staircase which I began to climb at top speed, mindless of my heart, like one hotly pursued by a homicidal maniac. This staircase faintly lit by I know not what means, slits perhaps, I mounted panting as far as the projecting gallery in which it culminated and which, separated from the void by a cynical parapet, encompassed a smooth round wall capped by a little dome covered with lead or verdigrised copper, phew, if that's not clear. People must have come here for the view, those who fall die on the way. Flattening myself against the wall I started round, clockwise. But I had hardly gone a few steps when I met a man revolving in the other direction, with the utmost circumspection. How I'd love to push him, or him to push me, over the edge. He gazed at me wild-eyed for a moment and then, not daring to pass me on the parapet side and surmising correctly that I would not relinquish the wall just to oblige him, abruptly turned his back on me, his head rather, for his back remained glued to the wall, and went back the way he had come so that soon there was nothing left of him but a left hand. It lingered a moment, then slid out of sight. All that remained to me was the vision of two burning eyes starting out of their sockets under a check cap. Into what nightmare thingness am I fallen? My hat flew off, but did not get far thanks to the string. I turned my head towards the staircase and lent an eye. Nothing. Then a little girl came into view followed by a man holding her by the hand, both pressed against the wall. He pushed her into the stairway, disappeared after her, turned and raised towards me a face that made me recoil. I could only see his bare head above the top step. When they were gone I called. I completed in haste the round of the gallery. No one. I saw on the horizon, where sky, sea, plain and mountain meet, a few low stars, not to be confused with the fires men light, at night, or that go alight alone. Enough.

Back in the street I tried to find my way in the sky, where I knew the Bears so well. If I had seen someone I would have stopped him to ask, the most ferocious aspect would not have daunted me. I would have said, touching my hat, Pardon me your honour, the Shepherds' Gate for the love of God. I thought I could go no further, but no sooner had the impetus reached my legs than on I went, believe it or not, at a very fair pace. I wasn't returning empty-handed, not quite, I was taking back with me the virtual certainty that I was still of this world, of that world too, in a way. But I was paying the price. I would have done better to spend the night in the cathedral, on the mat before the altar, I would have continued on my way at first light, or they would have found me stretched out in the rigor of death, the genuine bodily article, under the blue eyes fount of so much hope, and put me in the evening papers. But suddenly I was descending a wide street, vaguely familiar, but in which I could never have set foot, in my lifetime. But soon realizing I was going downhill I turned about and set off in the other direction. For I was afraid if I went downhill of returning to the sea where I had sworn never to return. When I say I turned about I mean I wheeled round in a wide semi-circle without slowing down, for I was afraid if I stopped of not being able to start again, yes, I was afraid of that too. And this evening too I dare not stop. I was struck more and more by the contrast between the brightly lit streets and their deserted air. To say it distressed me, no, but I say it all the same, in the hope of calming myself. To say there was no one abroad, no, I would not go that far, for I remarked a number of shapes, male and female, strange shapes, but not more so than usual. As to what hour it might have been I had no idea, except that it must have been some hour of the night. But it might have been three or four in the morning just as it might have been ten or eleven in the evening, depending no doubt on whether one wondered at the scarcity of passers-by or at the extraordinary radiance shed by the street-lamps and traffic-lights. For at one or other of these no one could fail to wonder, unless he was out of his mind. Not a single private car but admittedly from time to time a public vehicle, slow sweep of light silent and empty. It is not my wish to labour these antinomies, for we are needless to say in a skull, but I have no choice but to add the following few remarks. All the mortals I saw were alone and as if sunk in themselves. It must be a common sight but mixed with something else I imagine. The only couple was two men grappling, their legs intertwined. I only saw one cyclist! He was going the same way as I was. All were going the same way as I was, vehicles too, I have only just realized it. He was pedalling slowly in the middle of the street, reading a newspaper which he held with both hands spread open before his eyes. Every now and then he rang his bell without interrupting his reading. I watched him recede till he was no more than a dot on the horizon. Suddenly a young woman perhaps of easy virtue, dishevelled and her dress in disarray, darted across the street like a rabbit. That is all I had to add. But here a strange thing, yet another, I had no pain whatever, not even in my legs. Weakness. A good night's nightmare and a tin of sardines would restore my sensitivity. My shadow, one of my shadows, flew before me, dwindled, slid under my feet, trailed behind me the way shadows will. This degree of opacity appeared to me conclusive. But suddenly ahead of me a man on the same side of the street and going the same way, to keep harping on the same thing lest I forget. The distance between us was considerable, seventy paces at least, and fearing he might escape me I quickened my step with the result I swept forward as if on rollers. This is not me, I said, let us make the most of it. Finding myself in an instant a bare ten paces in his rear I slowed down so as not to burst in on him and so heighten the aversion my person inspired even in its most abject and obsequious attitudes. And a moment later, keeping humbly in step with him, Excuse me your honour, the Shepherds' Gate for the love of God! At close quarters he appeared normal apart from that air already noted of ebbing inward. I drew a few steps ahead, turned, cringed, touched my hat and said, The right time for mercy's sake! I might as well not have existed. But what about the sweet? A light! I cried. Given my need of help I can't think why I did not bar his path. I couldn't have, that's all, I couldn't have touched him. Seeing a stone seat by the kerb I sat down and crossed my legs, like Walther. I must have dozed off, for the next thing was a man sitting beside me. I was still taking him in when he opened his eyes and set them on me, as if for the first time, for he shrank back unaffectedly. Where did you spring from? he said. To hear myself addressed again so soon impressed me greatly. What's the matter with you? he said. I tried to look like one with whom that only is the matter which is native to him. Forgive me your honour, I said, gingerly lifting my hat and rising a fraction from the seat, the right time for the love of God! He said a time, I don't remember which, a time that explained nothing, that's all I remember, and did not calm me. But what time could have done that? Oh I know, I know, one will come that will. But in the meantime? What's that you said? he said. Unfortunately I had said nothing. But I wriggled out of it by asking him if he could help me find my way which I had lost. No, he said, for I am not from these parts and if I am sitting on this slab it is because the hotels were full or would not let me in, I have no opinion. But tell me the story of your life, then we'll see. My life! I cried. Why yes, he said, you know, that kind of – what shall I say? He brooded for a time, no doubt trying to think of what life could well be said to be a kind. In the end he went on, testily, Come now, everyone knows that. He jogged me in the ribs. No details, he said, the main drift, the main drift. But as I remained silent he said, Shall I tell you mine, then you'll see what I mean. The account he then gave was brief and dense, facts, without comment. That's what I call a life, he said, do you follow me now? It wasn't bad, his story, positively fairy-like in places. But that Pauline, I said, are you still with her? I am, he said, but I'm going to leave her and set up with another, younger and plumper. You travel a lot, I said. Oh widely, widely, he said. Words were coming back to me, and the way to make them sound. All that's a thing of the past for you no doubt, he said. Do you think of spending some time among us? I said. This sentence struck me as particularly well turned. If it's not a rude question, he said, how old are you? I don't know, I said. You don't know! he cried. Not exactly, I said. Are thighs much in your thoughts, he said, arses, cunts and environs? I didn't follow. No more erections naturally, he said. Erections? I said. The penis, he said, you know what the penis is, there, between the legs. Ah that! I said. It thickens, lengthens, stiffens and rises, he said, does it not? I assented, though they were not the terms I would have used. That is what we call an erection, he said. He pondered, then exclaimed, Phenomenal! No? Strange right enough, I said. And there you have it all, he said. But what will become of her? I said. Who? he said. Pauline, I said. She will grow old, he said with tranquil assurance, slowly at first, then faster and faster, in pain and bitterness, pulling the devil by the tail. The face was not full, but I eyed it in vain, it remained clothed in its flesh instead of turning all chalky and channelled as with a gouge. The very vomer kept its cushion. It is true discussion was always bad for me. I longed for the tender nonsuch, I would have trodden it gently, with my boots in my hand, and for the shade of my wood, far from this terrible light. What are you grinning and bearing? he said. He held on his knees a big black bag, like a midwife's I imagine. It was full of glittering phials. I asked him if they were all alike. Oho no, he said, for every taste. He took one and held it out to me, saying, One and six. What did he want? To sell it to me? Proceeding on this hypothesis I told him I had no money. No money! he cried. All of a sudden his hand came down on the back of my neck, his sinewy fingers closed and with a jerk and a twist he had me up against him. But instead of dispatching me he began to murmur words so sweet that I went limp and my head fell forward in his lap. Between the caressing voice and the fingers rowelling my neck the contrast was striking. But gradually the two things merged in a devastating hope, if I dare say so, and I dare. For this evening I have nothing to lose that I can discern. And if I have reached this point (in my story) without anything having changed, for if anything had changed I think I'd know, the fact remains I have reached it, and that's something, and with nothing changed, and that's something too. It's no excuse for rushing matters. No, it must cease gently, as gently cease on the stairs the steps of the loved one, who could not love and will not come back, and whose steps say so, that she could not love and will not come back. He suddenly shoved me away and showed me the phial again. There you have it all, he said. It can't have been the same all as before. Want it? he said. No, but I said yes, so as not to vex him. He proposed an exchange. Give me your hat, he said. I refused. What vehemence! he said. I haven't a thing, I said. Try in your pockets, he said. I haven't a thing, I said, I came out without a thing. Give me a lace, he said. I refused. Long silence. And if you gave me a kiss, he said finally. I knew there were kisses in the air. Can you take off your hat? he said. I took it off. Put it back, he said, you look nicer with it on. I put it back. Come on, he said, give me a kiss and let there be an end to it. Did it not occur to him I might turn him down? No, a kiss is not a bootlace, he must have seen from my face that all passion was not quite spent. Come, he said. I wiped my mouth in its tod of hair and advanced it towards his. Just a moment, he said. My mouth stood still. You know what a kiss is? he said. Yes yes, I said. If it's not a rude question, he said, when was your last? Some time ago, I said, but I can still do them. He took off his hat, a bowler, and tapped the middle of his forehead. There, he said, and there only. He had a noble brow, white and high. He leaned forward, closing his eyes. Quick, he said. I pursed up my lips as mother had taught me and brought them down where he had said. Enough, he said. He raised his hand to the spot, but left the gesture unfinished and put on his hat. I turned away and looked across the street. It was then I noticed we were sitting opposite a horse-butcher's. Here, he said, take it. I had forgotten. He rose. Standing he was quite short. One good turn, he said, with radiant smile. His teeth shone. I listened to his steps die away. How tell what remains? But it's the end. Or have I been dreaming, am I dreaming? No no, none of that, for dream is nothing, a joke, and significant what is worse. I said, Stay where you are till day breaks, wait sleeping till the lamps go out and the streets come to life. But I stood up and moved off. My pains were back, but with something untoward which prevented my wrapping them round me. But I said, Little by little you are coming to. From my gait alone, slow, stiff and which seemed at every step to solve a stato-dynamic problem never posed before, I would have been known again, if I had been known. I crossed over and stopped before the butcher's. Behind the grille the curtains were drawn, rough canvas curtains striped blue and white, colours of the Virgin, and stained with great pink stains. They did not quite meet in the middle, and through the chink I could make out the dim carcasses of the gutted horses hanging from hooks head downwards. I hugged the walls, famished for shadow. To think that in a moment all will be said, all to do again. And the city clocks, what was wrong with them, whose great chill clang even in my wood fell on me from the air? What else? Ah yes, my spoils. I tried to think of Pauline, but she eluded me, gleamed an instant and was gone, like the young woman in the street. So I went in the atrocious brightness, bedded in my old flesh, straining towards an issue and passing them by to left and right and my mind panting after this and that and always flung back to where there was nothing. I succeeded however in fastening briefly on the little girl, long enough to see her a little more clearly than before, so that she wore a kind of bonnet and clasped in her hand a book, of common prayer perhaps, and to try and have her smile, but she did not smile, but vanished down the staircase without having yielded me her little face. I had to stop. At first nothing, then little by little, I mean rising up out of the silence till suddenly no higher, a kind of massive murmur coming perhaps from the house that was propping me up. That reminded me that the houses were full of people, besieged, no, I don't know. When I stepped back to look at the windows I could see, in spite of shutters, blinds and muslins, that many of the rooms were lit. The light was so dimmed by the brilliancy flooding the boulevard that short of knowing or suspecting it was not so one might have supposed everyone sleeping. The sound was not continuous, but broken by silences possibly of consternation. I thought of ringing at the door and asking for shelter and protection till morning. But suddenly I was on my way again. But little by little, in a slow swoon, darkness fell about me. I saw a mass of bright flowers fade in an exquisite cascade of paling colours. I found myself admiring, all along the housefronts, the gradual blossoming of squares and rectangles, casement and sash, yellow, green, pink, according to the curtains and blinds, finding that pretty. Then at last, before I fell, first to my knees, as cattle do, then on my face, I was in a throng. I didn't lose consciousness, when I lose consciousness it will not be to recover it. They paid no heed to me, though careful not to walk on me, a courtesy that must have touched me, it was what I had come out for. It was well with me, sated with dark and calm, lying at the feet of mortals, fathom deep in the grey of dawn, if it was dawn. But reality, too tired to look for the right word, was soon restored, the throng fell away, the light came back and I had no need to raise my head from the ground to know I was back in the same blinding void as before. I said, Stay where you are, down on the friendly stone, or at least indifferent, don't open your eyes, wait for morning. But up with me again and back on the way that was not mine, on uphill along the boulevard. A blessing he was not waiting for me, poor old Breem, or Breen. I said, The sea is east, it's west I must go, to the left of north. But in vain I raised without hope my eyes to the sky to look for the Bears. For the light I steeped in put out the stars, assuming they were there, which I doubted, remembering the clouds.

Translated by the author

First Love

I associate, rightly or wrongly, my marriage with the death of my father, in time. That other links exist, on other levels, between these two affairs, is not impossible. I have enough trouble as it is in trying to say what I think I know.

I visited, not so long ago, my father's grave, that I do know, and noted the date of his death, of his death alone, for that of his birth had no interest for me, on that particular day. I set out in the morning and was back by night, having lunched lightly in the graveyard. But some days later, wishing to know his age at death, I had to return to the grave, to note the date of his birth. These two limiting dates I then jotted down on a piece of paper, which I now carry about with me. I am thus in a position to affirm that I must have been about twenty-five at the time of my marriage. For the date of my own birth, I repeat, my own birth, I have never forgotten, I never had to note it down, it remains graven in my memory, the year at least, in figures that life will not easily erase. The day itself comes back to me, when I put my mind to it, and I often celebrate it, after my fashion, I don't say each time it comes back, for it comes back too often, but often.

Personally I have no bone to pick with graveyards, I take the air there willingly, perhaps more willingly than elsewhere, when take the air I must. The smell of corpses, distinctly perceptible under those of grass and humus mingled, I do not find unpleasant, a trifle on the sweet side perhaps, a trifle heady, but how infinitely preferable to what the living emit, their feet, teeth, armpits, arses, sticky foreskins and frustrated ovules. And when my father's remains join in, however modestly, I can almost shed a tear. The living wash in vain, in vain perfume themselves, they stink. Yes, as a place for an outing, when out I must, leave me my graveyards and keep – you – to your public parks and beauty-spots. My sandwich, my banana, taste sweeter when I'm sitting on a tomb, and when the time comes to piss again, as it so often does, I have my pick. Or I wander, hands clasped behind my back, among the slabs, the flat, the leaning and the upright, culling the inscriptions. Of these I never weary, there are always three or four of such drollery that I have to hold on to the cross, or the stele, or the angel, so as not to fall. Mine I composed long since and am still pleased with it, tolerably pleased. My other writings are no sooner dry than they revolt me, but my epitaph still meets with my approval. There is little chance unfortunately of its ever being reared above the skull that conceived it, unless the State takes up the matter. But to be unearthed I must first be found, and I greatly fear those gentlemen will have as much trouble finding me dead as alive. So I hasten to record it here and now, while there is yet time:

> Hereunder lies the above who up below
> So hourly died that he lived on till now.

The second and last or rather latter line limps a little perhaps, but that is no great matter, I'll be forgiven more than that when I'm forgotten. Then with a little luck you hit on a genuine interment, with real live mourners and the odd relict trying to throw herself into the pit. And nearly always that charming business with the dust, though in my experience there is nothing less dusty than holes of this type, verging on muck for the most part, nor anything particularly powdery about the deceased, unless he happened to have died, or she, by fire. No matter, their little gimmick with the dust is charming. But my father's yard was not amongst my favourites. To begin with it was too remote, way out in the wilds of the country on the side of a hill, and too small, far too small, to go on with. Indeed it was almost full, a few more widows and they'd be turning them away. I infinitely preferred Ohlsdorf, particularly the Linne section, on Prussian soil, with its nine hundred acres of corpses packed tight, though I knew no one there, except by reputation the wild animal collector Hagenbeck. A lion, if I remember right, is carved on his monument, death must have had for Hagenbeck the countenance of a lion. Coaches ply to and fro, crammed with widows, widowers, orphans and the like. Groves, grottoes, artificial lakes with swans, offer consolation to the inconsolable. It was December, I had never felt so cold, the eel soup lay heavy on my stomach, I was afraid I'd die, I turned aside to vomit, I envied them.

But to pass on to less melancholy matters, on my father's death I had to leave the house. It was he who wanted me in the house. He was a strange man. One day he said, Leave him alone, he's not disturbing anyone. He didn't know I was listening. This was a view he must have often voiced, but the other times I wasn't by. They would never let me see his will, they simply said he had left me such a sum. I believed then and still believe he had stipulated in his will that I be left the room I had occupied in his lifetime and for food to be brought me there, as hitherto. He may even have given this the force of condition precedent. Presumably he liked to feel me under his roof, otherwise he would not have opposed my eviction. Perhaps he merely pitied me. But somehow I think not. He should have left me the entire house, then I'd have been all right, the others too for that matter, I'd have summoned them and said, Stay, stay by all means, your home is here. Yes, he was properly had, my poor father, if his purpose was really to go on protecting me from beyond the tomb. With regard to the money it is only fair to say they gave it to me without delay, on the very day following the inhumation. Perhaps they were legally bound to. I said to them, Keep this money and let me live on here, in my room, as in Papa's lifetime. I added, God rest his soul, in the hope of melting them. But they refused. I offered to place myself at their disposal, a few hours every day, for the little odd maintenance jobs every dwelling requires, if it is not to crumble away. Pottering is still just possible, I don't know why. I proposed in particular to look after the hothouse. There I would have gladly whiled away the hours, in the heat, tending the tomatoes, hyacinths, pinks and seedlings. My father and I alone, in that household, understood tomatoes. But they refused. One day, on my return from stool, I found my room locked and my belongings in a heap before the door. This will give you some idea how constipated I was, at this juncture. It was, I am now convinced, anxiety constipation. But was I genuinely constipated? Somehow I think not. Softly, softly. And yet I must have been, for how otherwise account for those long, those cruel sessions in the necessary house? At such times I never read, any more than at other times, never gave way to revery or meditation, just gazed dully at the almanac hanging from a nail before my eyes, with its chromo of a bearded stripling in the midst of sheep, Jesus no doubt, parted the cheeks with both hands and strained, heave! ho! heave! ho!, with the motions of one tugging at the oar, and only one thought in my mind, to be back in my room and flat on my back again. What can that have been but constipation? Or am I confusing it with diarrhoea? It's all a muddle in my head, graves and nuptials and the different varieties of motion. Of my scanty belongings they had made a little heap, on the floor, against the door. I can still see that little heap, in the kind of recess full of shadow between the landing and my room. It was in this narrow space, guarded on three sides only, that I had to change, I mean exchange my dressing-gown and nightgown for my travelling costume, I mean shoes, socks, trousers, shirt, coat, greatcoat and hat, I can think of nothing else. I tried other doors, turning the knobs and pushing, or pulling, before I left the house, but none yielded. I think if I'd found one open I'd have barricaded myself in the room, nothing less than gas would have dislodged me. I felt the house crammed as usual, the usual pack, but saw no one. I imagined them in their various rooms, all bolts drawn, every sense on the alert. Then the rush to the window, each holding back a little, hidden by the curtain, at the sound of the street door closing behind me, I should have left it open. Then the doors fly open and out they pour, men, women and children, and the voices, the sighs, the smiles, the hands, the keys in the hands, the blessed relief, the precautions rehearsed, if this then that, but if that then this, all clear and joy in every heart, come let's eat, the fumigation can wait. All imagination to be sure, I was already on my way, things may have passed quite differently, but who cares how things pass, provided they pass. All those lips that had kissed me, those hearts that had loved me (it is with the heart one loves, is it not, or am I confusing it with something else?), those hands that had played with mine and those minds that had almost made their own of me! Humans are truly strange. Poor Papa, a nice mug he must have felt that day if he could see me, see us, a nice mug on my account I mean. Unless in his great disembodied wisdom he saw further than his son whose corpse was not yet quite up to scratch.

But to pass on to less melancholy matters, the name of the

woman with whom I was soon to be united was Lulu. So at least she assured me and I can't see what interest she could have had in lying to me, on this score. Of course one can never tell. She also disclosed her family name, but I've forgotten it. I should have made a note of it, on a piece of paper, I hate to forget a proper name. I met her on a bench, on the bank of the canal, one of the canals, for our town boasts two, though I never knew which was which. It was a well situated bench, backed by a mound of solid earth and garbage, so that my rear was covered. My flanks too, partially, thanks to a pair of venerable trees, more than venerable, dead, at either end of the bench. It was no doubt these trees one fine day, aripple with all their foliage, that had sown the idea of a bench, in someone's fancy. To the fore, a few yards away, flowed the canal, if canals flow, don't ask me, so that from that quarter too the risk of surprise was small. And yet she surprised me. I lay stretched out, the night being warm, gazing up through the bare boughs interlocking high above me, where the trees clung together for support, and through the drifting cloud, at a patch of starry sky as it came and went. Shove up, she said. My first movement was to go, but my fatigue, and my having nowhere to go, dissuaded me from acting on it. So I drew back my feet a little way and she sat. Nothing more passed between us that evening and she soon took herself off, without another word. All she had done was sing, beneath her breath, as to herself, and without the words fortunately, some old folk songs, and so disjointedly, skipping from one to another and finishing none, that even I found it strange. The voice, though out of tune, was not unpleasant. It breathed of a soul too soon wearied ever to conclude, that perhaps least arse-aching soul of all. The bench itself was soon more than she could bear and as for me, one look had been enough for her. Whereas in reality she was a most tenacious woman. She came back next day and the day after and all went off more or less as before. Perhaps a few words were exchanged. The next day it was raining and I felt in security. Wrong again. I asked her if she was resolved to disturb me every evening. I disturb you? she said. I felt her eyes on me. They can't have seen much, two eyelids at the most, with a hint of nose and brow, darkly, because of the dark. I thought we were easy, she said. You disturb me, I said, I can't stretch out with you there. The collar of my greatcoat was over my mouth and yet she heard me. Must you stretch out? she said. The mistake one makes is to speak to people. You have only to put your feet on my knees, she said. I didn't wait to be asked twice, under my miserable calves I felt her fat thighs. She began stroking my ankles. I considered kicking her in the cunt. You speak to people about stretching out and they immediately see a body at full length. What mattered to me in my dispeopled kingdom, that in regard to which the disposition of my carcass was the merest and most futile of accidents, was supineness in the mind, the dulling of the self and of that residue of execrable frippery known as the non-self and even the world, for short. But man is still today, at the age of twenty-five, at the mercy of an erection, physically too, from time to time, it's the common lot, even I was not immune, if that may be called an erection. It did not escape her naturally, women smell a rigid phallus ten miles away and wonder, How on earth did he spot me from there? One is no longer oneself, on such occasions, and it is painful to be no longer oneself, even more painful if possible than when one is. For when one is one knows what to do to be less so, whereas when one is not one is any old one irredeemably. What goes by the name of love is banishment, with now and then a postcard from the homeland, such is my considered opinion, this evening. When she had finished and my self been resumed, mine own, the mitigable, with the help of a brief torpor, it was alone. I sometimes wonder if that is not all invention, if in reality things did not take quite a different course, one I had no choice but to forget. And yet her image remains bound, for me, to that of the bench, not the bench by day, nor yet the bench by night, but the bench at evening, in such sort that to speak of the bench, as it appeared to me at evening, is to speak of her, for me. That proves nothing, but there is nothing I wish to prove. On the subject of the bench by day no words need be wasted, it never knew me, gone before morning and never back till dusk. Yes, in the daytime I foraged for food and marked down likely cover. Were you to inquire, as undoubtedly you itch, what I had done with the money my father had left me, the answer would be I had done nothing with it but leave it lie in my pocket. For I knew I would not be always young, and that summer does not last for ever either, nor even autumn, my mean soul told me so. In the end I told her I'd had enough. She disturbed me exceedingly, even absent. Indeed she still disturbs me, but no worse now than the rest. And it matters nothing to me now, to be disturbed, or so little, what does it mean, disturbed, and what would I do with myself if I wasn't? Yes, I've changed my system, it's the winning one at last, for the ninth or tenth time, not to mention not long now, not long till curtain down, on disturbers and disturbed, no more tattle about that, all that, her and the others, the shitball and heaven's high halls. So you don't want me to come any more, she said. It's incredible the way they repeat what you've just said to them, as if they risked faggot and fire in believing their ears. I told her to come just the odd time. I didn't understand women at that period. I still don't for that matter. Nor men either. Nor animals either. What I understand best, which is not saying much, are my pains. I think them through daily, it doesn't take long, thought moves so fast, but they are not only in my thought, not all.

Yes, there are moments, particularly in the afternoon, when I go all syncretist, à la Reinhold. What equilibrium! But even them, my pains, I understand ill. That must come from my not being all pain and nothing else. There's the rub. Then they recede, or I, till they fill me with amaze and wonder, seen from a better planet. Not often, but I ask no more. Catch-cony life! To be nothing but pain, how that would simplify matters! Omnidolent! Impious dream. I'll tell them to you some day none the less, if I think of it, if I can, my strange pains, in detail, distinguishing between the different kinds, for the sake of clarity, those of the mind, those of the heart or emotional conative, those of the soul (none prettier than these) and finally those of the frame proper, first the inner or latent, then those affecting the surface, beginning with the hair and scalp and moving methodically down, without haste, all the way down to the feet beloved of the corn, the cramp, the kibe, the bunion, the hammer toe, the nail ingrown, the fallen arch, the common blain, the club foot, duck foot, goose foot, pigeon foot, flat foot, trench foot and other curiosities. And I'll tell by the same token, for those kind enough to listen, in accordance with a system whose inventor I forget, of those instants when, neither drugged, nor drunk, nor in ecstasy, one feels nothing. Next of course she desired to know what I meant by the odd time, that's what you get for opening your mouth. Once a week? Once in ten days? Once a fortnight? I replied less often, far less often, less often to the point of no more if she could, and if she could not the least often possible. And the next day (what is more) I abandoned the bench, less I must confess on her account than on its, for the site no longer answered my requirements, modest though they were, now that the air was beginning to strike chill, and for other reasons better not wasted on cunts like you, and took refuge in a deserted cowshed marked on one of my forays. It stood in the corner of a field richer on the surface in nettles than in grass and in mud than in nettles, but whose subsoil was perhaps possessed of exceptional qualities. It was in this byre, littered with dry and hollow cowclaps subsiding with a sigh at the poke of my finger, that for the first time in my life, and I would not hesitate to say the last if I had not to husband my cyanide, I had to contend with a feeling which gradually assumed, to my dismay, the dread name of love. What constitutes the charm of our country, apart of course from its scant population, and this without help of the meanest contraceptive, is that all is derelict, with the sole exception of history's ancient faeces. These are ardently sought after, stuffed and carried in procession. Wherever nauseated time has dropped a nice fat turd you will find our patriots, sniffing it up on all fours, their faces on fire. Elysium of the roofless. Hence my happiness at last. Lie down, all seems to say, lie down and stay down. I see no connexion between these remarks. But that one exists, and even more than one, I have little doubt, for my part. But what? Which? Yes, I loved her, it's the name I gave, still give alas, to what I was doing then. I had nothing to go by, having never loved before, but of course had heard of the thing, at home, in school, in brothel and at church, and read romances, in prose and verse, under the guidance of my tutor, in six or seven languages, both dead and living, in which it was handled at length. I was therefore in a position, in spite of all, to put a label on what I was about when I found myself inscribing the letters of Lulu in an old heifer pat or flat on my face in the mud under the moon trying to tear up the nettles by the roots. They were giant nettles some full three foot high, to tear them up assuaged my pain, and yet it's not like me to do that to weeds, on the contrary, I'd smother them in manure if I had any. Flowers are a different matter. Love brings out the worst in man and no error. But what kind of love was this, exactly? Love-passion?

Somehow I think not. That's the priapic one, is it not? Or is this a different variety? There are so many, are there not? All equally if not more delicious, are they not? Platonic love, for example, there's another just occurs to me. It's disinterested. Perhaps I loved her with a platonic love? But somehow I think not. Would I have been tracing her name in old cowshit if my love had been pure and disinterested? And with my devil's finger into the bargain, which I then sucked. Come now! My thoughts were all of Lulu, if that doesn't give you some idea nothing will. Anyhow I'm sick and tired of this name Lulu, I'll give her another, more like her, Anna for example, it's not more like her but no matter. I thought of Anna then, I who had learnt to think of nothing, nothing except my pains, a quick think through, and of what steps to take not to perish off-hand of hunger, or cold, or shame, but never on any account of living beings as such (I wonder what that means) whatever I may have said, or may still say, to the contrary or otherwise, on this subject. But I have always spoken, no doubt always shall, of things that never existed, or that existed if you insist, no doubt always will, but not with the existence I ascribe to them. Kepis, for example, exist beyond a doubt, indeed there is little hope of their ever disappearing, but personally I never wore a kepi. I wrote somewhere, They gave me . . . a hat. Now the truth is they never gave me a hat, I have always had my own hat, the one my father gave me, and I have never had any other hat than that hat. I may add it has followed me to the grave. I thought of Anna then, long long sessions, twenty minutes, twenty-five minutes and even as long as half an hour daily. I obtain these figures by the addition of other, lesser figures. That must have been my way of loving. Are we to infer from this I loved her with that intellectual love which drew from me such drivel, in another place? Somehow I think not. For had my love been of this kind would I have stooped to inscribe the letters of Anna in time's forgotten cowpats? To divellicate urtica *plenis manibus*? And felt, under my tossing head, her thighs to bounce like so many demon bolsters? Come now! In order to put an end, to try and put an end, to this plight, I returned one evening to the bench, at the hour she had used to join me there. There was no sign of her and I waited in vain. It was December already, if not January, and the cold was seasonable, that is to say reasonable, like all that is seasonable. But one is the hour of the dial, and another that of changing air and sky, and another yet again the heart's. To this thought, once back in the straw, I owed an excellent night. The next day I was earlier to the bench, much earlier, night having barely fallen, winter night, and yet too late, for she was there already, on the bench, under the boughs tinkling with rime, her back to the frosted mound, facing the icy water. I told you she was a highly tenacious woman. I felt nothing. What interest could she have in pursuing me thus? I asked her, without sitting down, stumping to and fro. The cold had embossed the path. She replied she didn't know. What could she see in me, would she kindly tell me that at least, if she could. She replied she couldn't. She seemed warmly clad, her hands buried in a muff. As I looked at this muff, I remember, tears came to my eyes. And yet I forget what colour it was. The state I was in then! I have always wept freely, without the least benefit to myself, till recently. If I had to weep this minute I could squeeze till I was blue, I'm convinced not a drop would fall. The state I am in now! It was things made me weep. And yet I felt no sorrow. When I found myself in tears for no apparent reason it meant I had caught sight of something unbeknownst. So I wonder if it was really the muff that evening, if it was not rather the path, so iron hard and bossy as perhaps to feel like cobbles to my tread, or some other thing, some chance thing glimpsed below the threshold, that so unmanned me. As for her, I might as well never have laid eyes on her before. She sat all huddled and muffled up, her head sunk, the muff with her hands in her lap, her legs pressed tight together, her heels clear of the ground. Shapeless, ageless, almost lifeless, it might have been anything or anyone, an old woman or a little girl. And the way she kept on saying, I don't know, I can't. I alone did not know and could not. Is it on my account you came? I said. She managed yes to that. Well here I am, I said. And I? Had I not come on hers? Here we are, I said. I sat down beside her but sprang up again immediately as though scalded. I longed to be gone, to know if it was over. But before going, to be on the safe side, I asked her to sing me a song. I thought at first she was going to refuse, I mean simply not sing, but no, after a moment she began to sing and sang for some time, all the time the same song it seemed to me, without change of attitude. I did not know the song, I had never heard it before and shall never hear it again. It had something to do with lemon trees, or orange trees, I forget, that is all I remember, and for me that is no mean feat, to remember it had something to do with lemon trees, or orange trees, I forget, for of all the other songs I have ever heard in my life, and I have heard plenty, it being apparently impossible, physically impossible short of being deaf, to get through this world, even my way, without hearing singing, I have retained nothing, not a word, not a note, or so few words, so few notes, that, that what, that nothing, this sentence has gone on long enough. Then I started to go and as I went I heard her singing another song, or perhaps more verses of the same, fainter and fainter the further I went, then no more, either because she had come to an end or because I was gone too far to hear her. To have to harbour such a doubt was something I preferred to avoid, at that period. I lived of course in doubt, on doubt, but such trivial doubts as this, purely somatic as some say, were best cleared up without delay, they could nag at me like gnats for weeks on end. So I retraced my steps a little way and stopped. At first I heard nothing, then the voice again, but only just, so faintly did it carry. First I didn't hear it, then I did, I must therefore have begun hearing it, at a certain point, but no, there was no beginning, the sound emerged so softly from the silence and so resembled it. When the voice ceased at last I approached a little nearer, to make sure it had really ceased and not merely been lowered. Then in despair, saying, No knowing, no knowing, short of being beside her, bent over her, I turned on my heel and went, for good, full of doubt. But some weeks later, even more dead than alive than usual I returned to the bench, for the fourth or fifth time since I had abandoned it, at roughly the same hour, I mean roughly the same sky, no, I don't mean that either, for it's always the same sky and never the same sky, what words are there for that, none I know, period. She wasn't there, then suddenly she was, I don't know how, I didn't see her come, nor hear her, all ears and eyes though I was. Let us say it was raining, nothing like a change, if only of weather. She had her umbrella up, naturally, what an outfit. I asked if she came every evening. No, she said, just the odd time. The bench was soaking wet, we paced up and down, not daring to sit. I took her arm, out of curiosity, to see if it would give me pleasure, it gave me none, I let it go. But why these particulars? To put off the evil hour. I saw her face a little clearer, it seemed normal to me, a face like millions of others. The eyes were crooked, but I didn't know that till later. It looked neither young nor old, the face, as though stranded between the vernal and the sere. Such ambiguity I found difficult to bear, at that period. As to whether it was beautiful, the face, or had once been beautiful, or could conceivably become beautiful, I confess I could form no opinion. I had seen faces in photographs I might have found beautiful had I known even vaguely in what beauty was supposed to consist. And my father's face, on his death-bolster, had seemed to hint at some form of aesthetics relevant to man. But the faces of the living, all grimace and flush, can they be described as objects? I admired in spite of the dark, in spite of my fluster, the way still or scarcely flowing water reaches up, as though athirst, to that falling from the sky. She asked if I would like her to sing something. I replied no, I would like her to say something. I thought she would say she had nothing to say, it would have been like her, and so was agreeably surprised when she said she had a room, most agreeably surprised, though I suspected as much. Who has not a room? Ah I hear the clamour. I have two rooms, she said. Just how many rooms do you have? I said. She said she had two rooms and a kitchen. The premises were expanding steadily, given time she would remember a bathroom. Is it two rooms I heard you say? I said. Yes, she said. Adjacent? I said. At last conversation worthy of the name. Separated by the kitchen, she said. I asked her why she had not told me before. I must have been beside myself, at this period. I did not feel easy when I was with her, but at least free to think of something else than her, of the old trusty things, and so little by little, as down steps towards a deep, of nothing. And I knew that away from her I would forfeit this freedom.

There were in fact two rooms, separated by a kitchen, she had not lied to me. She said I should have fetched my things. I explained I had no things. It was at the top of an old house, with a view of the mountains for those who cared. She lit an oil-lamp. You have no current? I said. No, she said, but I have running water and gas. Ha, I said, you have gas. She began to undress. When at their wit's end they undress, no doubt the wisest course. She took off everything, with a slowness fit to enflame an elephant, except her stockings, calculated presumably to bring my concupiscence to the boil. It was then I noticed the squint. Fortunately she was not the first naked woman to have crossed my path, so I could stay, I knew she would not explode. I asked to see the other room which I had not yet seen. If I had seen it already I would have asked to see it again. Will you not undress? she said. Oh you know, I said, I seldom undress. It was the truth, I was never one to undress indiscriminately. I often took off my boots when I went to bed, I mean when I composed myself (composed!) to sleep, not to mention this or that outer garment according to the outer temperature. She was therefore obliged, out of common savoir faire, to throw on a wrap and light me the way. We went via the kitchen. We could just as well have gone via the corridor, as I realized later, but we went via the kitchen, I don't know why, perhaps it was the shorter way. I surveyed the room with horror. Such density of furniture defeats imagination. Not a doubt, I must have seen that room somewhere. What's this? I cried. The parlour, she said. The parlour! I began putting out the furniture through the door to the corridor. She watched, in sorrow I suppose, but not necessarily. She asked me what I was doing. She can't have expected an answer. I put it out piece by piece, and even two at a time, and stacked it all up in the corridor, against the outer wall. There were hundreds of pieces, large and small, in the end they blocked the door, making egress impossible, and *a fortiori* ingress, to and from the corridor. The door could be opened and closed, since it opened inwards, but had become impassable. To put it mildly. At least take off your hat, she said. I'll treat of my hat some other time perhaps. Finally the room was empty but for a sofa and some shelves fixed to the wall. The former I dragged to the back of the room, near the door, and next day took down the latter and put them out, in the corridor, with the rest. As I was taking them down, strange memory, I heard the word fibrome, or brone, I don't know which, never knew, never knew what it meant and never had the curiosity to find out. The things one recalls! And records! When all was in order at last I dropped on the sofa. She had not raised her little finger to help me. I'll get sheets and blankets, she said. But I wouldn't hear of sheets. You couldn't draw the curtain? I said. The window was frosted over. The effect was not white, because of the night, but faintly luminous none the less. This faint cold sheen, though I lay with my feet towards the door, was more than I could bear. I suddenly rose and changed the position of the sofa, that is to say turned it round so that the back, hitherto against the wall, was now on the outside and consequently the front, or way in, on the inside. Then I climbed back, like a dog into its basket. I'll leave you the lamp, she said, but I begged her to take it with her. And suppose you need something in the night, she said. She was going to start quibbling again, I could feel it. Do you know where the convenience is? she said. She was right, I was forgetting. To relieve oneself in bed is enjoyable at the time, but soon a source of discomfort. Give me a chamber-pot, I said. But she did not possess one. I have a close-stool of sorts, she said. I saw the grandmother on it, sitting up very stiff and grand, having just purchased it, pardon, picked it up, at a charity sale, or perhaps won it in a raffle, a period piece, and now trying it out, doing her best rather, almost wishing someone could see her. That's the idea, procrastinate. Any old recipient, I said, I don't have the flux. She came back with a kind of saucepan, not a true saucepan for it had no handle, it was oval in shape with two lugs and a lid. My stewpan, she said. I don't need the lid, I said. You don't need the lid? she said. If I had needed the lid she would have said, You need the lid? I drew this utensil down under the blanket, I like something in my hand when sleeping, it reassures me, and my hat was still wringing. I turned to the wall. She caught up the lamp off the mantelpiece where she had set it down, that's the idea, every particular, it flung her waving shadow over me, I thought she was off, but no, she came stooping down towards me over the sofa back. All family possessions, she said. I in her shoes would have tiptoed away, but not she, not a stir. Already my love was waning, that was all that mattered. Yes, already I felt better, soon I'd be up to the slow descents again, the long submersions, so long denied me through her fault. And I had only just moved in! Try and put me out now, I said. I seemed not to grasp the meaning of these words, nor even hear the brief sound they made, till some seconds after having uttered them. I was so unused to speech that my mouth would sometimes open, of its own accord, and vent some phrase or phrases, grammatically unexceptionable but entirely devoid if not of meaning, for on close inspection they would reveal one, and even several, at least of foundation. But I heard each word no sooner spoken. Never had my voice taken so long to reach me as on this occasion. I turned over on my back to see what was going on. She was smiling. A little later she went away, taking the lamp with her. I heard her steps in the kitchen and then the door of her room close behind her. Why behind her? I was alone at last, in the dark at last. Enough about that. I thought I was all set for a good night, in spite of the strange surroundings, but no, my night was most agitated. I woke next morning quite worn out, my clothes in disorder, the blanket likewise, and Anna beside me, naked naturally. One shudders to think of her exertions. I still had the stewpan in my grasp. It had not served. I looked at my member. If only it could have spoken! Enough about that. It was my night of love.

Gradually I settled down, in this house. She brought my meals at the appointed hours, looked in now and then to see if all was well and make sure I needed nothing, emptied the stewpan once a day and did out the room once a month. She could not always resist the temptation to speak to me, but on the whole gave me no cause to complain. Sometimes I heard her singing in her room, the song traversed her door, then the kitchen, then my door, and in this way won to me, faint but indisputable. Unless it travelled by the corridor. This did not greatly incommode me, this occasional sound of singing. One day I asked her to bring me a hyacinth, live, in a pot. She brought it and put it on the mantelpiece, now the only place in my room to put things, unless you put them on the floor. Not a day passed without my looking at it. At first all went well, it even put forth a bloom or two, then it gave up and was soon no more than a limp stem hung with limp leaves. The bulb, half clear of the clay as though in search of oxygen, smelt foul. She wanted to remove it, but I told her to leave it. She wanted to get me another, but I told her I didn't want another. I was more seriously disturbed by other sounds, stifled giggles and groans, which filled the dwelling at certain hours of the night, and even of the day. I had given up thinking of her, quite given up, but still I needed silence, to live my life. In vain I tried to listen to such reasonings as that air is made to carry the clamours of the world, including inevitably much groan and giggle, I obtained no relief. I couldn't make out if it was always the same gent or more than one. Lovers' groans are so alike, and lovers' giggles. I had such horror then of these paltry perplexities that I always fell into the same error, that of seeking to clear them up. It took me a long time, my lifetime so to speak, to realize that the colour of an eye half seen, or the source of some distant sound, are closer to Giudecca in the hell of unknowing than the existence of God, or the origins of protoplasm, or the existence of self, and even less worthy than these to occupy the wise. It's a bit much, a lifetime, to achieve this consoling conclusion, it doesn't leave you much time to profit by it. So a fat lot of help it was when, having put the question to her, I was told they were clients she received in rotation. I could obviously have got up and gone to look through the keyhole. But what can you see, I ask you, through holes the likes of those? So you live by prostitution, I said. We live by prostitution, she said. You couldn't ask them to make less noise? I said, as if I believed her. I added, Or a different kind of noise. They can't help but yap and yelp, she said. I'll have to leave, I said. She found some old hangings in the family junk and hung them before our doors, hers and mine. I asked her if it would not be possible, now and then, to have a parsnip. A parsnip! she cried, as if I had asked for a dish of sucking Jew. I reminded her that the parsnip season was fast drawing to a close and that if, before it finally got there, she could feed me nothing but parsnips I'd be grateful. I like parsnips because they taste like violets and violets because they smell like parsnips. Were there no parsnips on earth violets would leave me cold and if violets did not exist I would care as little for parsnips as I do for turnips, or radishes. And even in the present state of their flora, I mean on this planet where parsnips and violets contrive to coexist, I could do without both with the utmost ease, the uttermost ease. One day she had the impudence to announce she was with child, and four or five months gone into the bargain, by me of all people! She offered me a side view of her belly. She even undressed, no doubt to prove she wasn't hiding a cushion under her skirt, and then of course for the pure pleasure of undressing. Perhaps it's just wind, I said, by way of consolation. She gazed at me with her big eyes whose colour I forget, with one big eye rather, for the other seemed riveted on the remains of the hyacinth. The more naked she was the more cross-eyed. Look, she said, stooping over her breasts, the haloes are darkening already. I summoned up my remaining strength and said, Abort, abort, and they'll blush like new. She had drawn back the curtain for a clear view of all her rotundities. I saw the mountain, impassible, cavernous, secret, where from morning to night I'd hear nothing but the wind, the curlews, the clink like distant silver of the stone-cutters' hammers. I'd come out in the daytime to the heather and gorse, all warmth and scent, and watch at night the distant city lights, if I chose, and the other lights, the lighthouses and lightships my father had named for me, when I was small, and whose names I could find again, in my memory, if I chose, that I knew. From that day forth things went from bad to worse, to worse and worse. Not that she neglected me, she could never have neglected me enough, but the way she kept plaguing me with *our* child, exhibiting her belly and breasts and saying it was due any moment, she could feel it lepping already. If it's lepping, I said, it's not mine. I might have been worse off than I was, in that house, that was certain, it fell short of my ideal naturally, but I wasn't blind to its advantages. I hesitated to leave, the leaves were falling already, I dreaded the winter. One should not dread the winter, it too has its bounties, the snow gives warmth and deadens the tumult and its pale days are soon over. But I did not yet know, at that time, how tender the earth can be for those who have only her and how many graves in her giving, for the living. What finished me was the birth. It woke me up. What that infant must have been going through! I fancy she had a woman with her, I seemed to hear steps in the kitchen, on and off. It went to my heart to leave a house without being put out. I crawled out over the back of the sofa, put on my coat, greatcoat and hat, I can think of nothing else, laced up my boots and opened the door to the corridor. A mass of junk barred my way, but I scrabbled and barged my way through it in the end, regardless of the clatter.

I used the word marriage, it was a kind of union in spite of all. Precautions would have been superfluous, there was no competing with those cries. It must have been her first. They pursued me down the stairs and out into the street. I stopped before the house door and listened. I could still hear them. If I had not known there was crying in the house I might not have heard them. But knowing it I did. I was not sure where I was. I looked among the stars and constellations for the Wains, but could not find them. And yet they must have been there. My father was the first to show them to me. He had shown me others, but alone, without him beside me, I could never find any but the Wains. I began playing with the cries, a little in the same way as I had played with the song, on, back, on, back, if that may be called playing. As long as I kept walking I didn't hear them, because of the footsteps. But as soon as I halted I heard them again, a little fainter each time, admittedly, but what does it matter, faint or loud, cry is cry, all that matters is that it should cease. For years I thought they would cease. Now I don't think so any more. I could have done with other loves perhaps. But there it is, either you love or you don't.

Notes

The first of Beckett's novellas to appear in print in English was *The End*, translated in collaboration with Richard Seaver and published in *Merlin*, No. 2, Summer–Autumn (Paris, 1954). Beckett entirely reworked this translation for the novella's publication in *Evergreen Review*, November–December (New York, 1960). *The Expelled* first appeared in *Evergreen Review*, No. 6, January–February (New York, 1962), and *The Calmative* in *Evergreen Review*, Vol. 11, No. 47 (New York, June 1967). Where appropriate these are cited in the Notes as *Evergreen*. The three novellas appeared together in *Stories and Texts for Nothing* (Grove Press, New York, 1967), cited in the Notes as Grove 67.

These three novellas first appeared in Britain in *No's Knife: Collected Shorter Prose 1945–1966* (Calder & Boyars, London, 1967, reprinted 1975), cited in the Notes as *No's Knife*. The fourth novella, *First Love*, first appeared in Britain in book form as *First Love* (Calder & Boyars, London, 1973), cited in the Notes as Calder 73, and in America as *First Love and Other Shorts* (Grove Press, New York, 1974), cited in the Notes as Grove 74. The four novellas together first appeared in Britain as *Four Novellas* (John Calder, London, 1977), cited in the Notes as Calder 77, and subsequently in *Collected Shorter Prose 1945–1980* (John Calder, London, 1984), cited in the Notes as *CSP*.

The first American gathering of the four novellas appeared in *The Complete Short Prose 1929–1989*, edited and with an Introduction and Notes by S. E. Gontarski (Grove Press, New York, 1995), cited in the Notes as Gontarski 95.

The pre-publication documentary record for the novellas in English is quite rich. The Olin Library, Washington University, St Louis, Missouri, holds a copy of the manuscript (cited as Ms), Typescript I (Ts 1) and Typescript II (Ts 2) of *The Calmative*. A second copy of Ts 2, also held there, has been marked up with instructions for printing. There are occasional corrections on this copy which do not feature on Ts 2 but which were carried over to the first printing of the novella in *Evergreen Review*. Similarly, the manuscript translation and two typescripts of *First Love* are held at Reading University Library where they are catalogued as MS 1227/7/14/1, 2 and 3 respectively (cited in the Notes as Ms, Ts 1 and Ts 2).

The French language original versions of three of the novellas, *La Fin*, *L'Expulsé* and *Le Calmant* were published in *Nouvelles et Textes pour rien* (Les Éditions de Minuit, Paris, 1958, reprinted 1987), cited in the Notes as *Nouvelles*. The fourth novella appeared as *Premier Amour* (Les Éditions de Minuit, Paris, 1970), cited in the Notes as Minuit 70.

Unless otherwise identified, ellipses in the Notes are editorial.

The End

(p. 9) *or profit by the collar*: Between *Evergreen* and Grove 67 Beckett revised the translation at this point. *Nouvelles* (p. 72) gives *Surtout la chemise, dont pendant longtemps je ne pouvais fermer le col, ni par conséquent arborer le faux-col, ni réunir les pans, avec une épingle, entre mes jambes, comme ma mère me l'avait montré. Evergreen* gives: *and it was many a long day before I could button it at the neck, or sport the collar that went with it . . .*

(p. 10) *with kinds of little stars*: *Evergreen* gives *It was blue, with sort of little stars on it*. This version is a more literal translation of the original: *Elle était bleue, avec comme des petites étoiles dessus. Nouvelles*, p. 73.

(p. 10) *I didn't feel well*: *Evergreen* gives *I didn't feel very well*.

(p. 10) *You might have left me in the bed*: All American printings, with the exception of Gontarski 95, give *You might have left me in bed . . .*

(p. 11) *When it is gone you will have to get more, if you want to go on*: All American printings, with the exception of Gontarski 95, give *When it is gone you will have to get more, if you wish to go on.*
(p. 12) The *loiter/cloister* pairing translates a *plus/pleut/plus* constellation in the original French: *Vous ne devez plus vous attarder dans le cloître maintenant qu'il ne pleut plus. Nouvelles*, p. 76.
(p. 12) *asked his mother how such a thing was possible*: An earlier version appears in *Evergreen – . . . asked his mother how that was possible.*
(p. 12) American printings, with the exception of Gontarski 95, offer a different pattern of punctuation: *I had as a matter of fact thought of it during our conversation in the hall. I had said to myself, Let us first finish our conversation, then I'll ask*. This pattern conforms more closely to that of *Nouvelles*, p. 77: *J'y avais bien pensé pendant notre conversation, dans le vestibule. Je me disais, Finissons d'abord ce que nous sommes en train de nous dire, puis je demanderai.*
(p. 14) *held it a second poised in such a way*: *Evergreen* gives *placed.*
(p. 14) *that the person addressed*: *Evergreen* gives *the person to whom I was speaking.*
(p. 14) *by wearing a kepi*: *Nouvelles* (p. 80) gives this as *un vieux kepi britannique. Evergreen* translates this as *a British kepi.*
(p. 15) *which she slipped over her arm*: *Evergreen* gives this as *hand.*
(p. 16) *of the woman passing by: Nouvelles* (p. 83) contains an additional sentence which does not appear in any printings of Beckett's translation: *Plus d'une jambe me devint ainsi familière.*
(p. 17) *something of that kind*: The original French (*Nouvelles*, p. 85) is significantly different – *Je ne dois pas me tromper de beaucoup.*
(p. 17) *no later than yesterday afternoon*: *Nouvelles* (p. 86) gives instead *pas plus tard qu'hier matin.*
(p. 18) *I think a kind of curry-comb*: *Evergreen* gives *I think it was a kind of curry-comb.*
(p. 18) *in the city*: *Evergreen* gives *town* instead of *city* in this and the next sentence.
(p. 18) *with a briefcase under his arm*: *Evergreen* gives *satchel* here – the original is *une serviette* (*Nouvelles*, p. 89); the revision to *briefcase* connects the son more directly to the bloom of adulthood (with hat and baldness) rather than to schooldays.

(p. 20) *My host was out*: *Nouvelles* (p. 92) gives this as *L'autre*.
(p. 20) *You wouldn't know of a lake dwelling*: *Nouvelles* (p. 92) gives this as *une caverne lacustre*.
(p. 20) *in my cabin in the mountains I was wretched*: American printings, with the exception of Gontarski 95, offer *in my cabin in the mountains I was very unhappy*. *Nouvelles* (p. 92) gives *j'étais très malheureux*.
(p. 21) *a little decayed no doubt*: *Evergreen* gives this as *dilapidated*.
(p. 21) *saying I had other plans*: *Evergreen* offers *saying I had made other arrangements*.
(p. 21) *The floor was strewn with excrements*: The original French is a trifle more specific – *Des excréments jonchaient le sol, d'homme, de vache, de chien, ainsi que des préservatifs et des vomissures* (*Nouvelles*, p. 93).
(p. 21) *No matter, it's free*: *Evergreen* offers *it's for nothing*.
(p. 22) *showing the stars and the distaff*: *Evergreen* offers *containing*.
(p. 22) *too far gone for the old trick*: *Evergreen* offers *the old turn*.
(p. 22) *My hour was not yet come*: *Evergreen* offers *had*.
(p. 22) *with one wheel at least, or two if there were four*: Subsequent to its first appearance in *Evergreen* Beckett deleted a brief passage from the translation: *The town planner with the red beard, they removed his gall-bladder, a gross mistake, and three days later he died, in the prime of life*. *Nouvelles* (p. 96) reads: *L'urbaniste à la barbe rouge, on lui enleva la vésicule biliaire, une grosse faute, et trois jours après il mourait, dans la force de l'âge*.
(p. 23) *the* Ethics *of Geulincx*: A certain instability attaches to the spelling of this name in Beckett's work; in some printings it is given as 'Geulincz'. The form used here conforms to that used in the earlier *Murphy* (1938, French translation 1947).
(p. 23) *on the fly-leaf*: *Evergreen* offers *front page*.
(p. 23) *but I had to make do with it*: *Evergreen* offers *but I had to put up with it*.
(p. 23) *he was in danger of touching me*: *Evergreen* offers *he risked touching me*.
(p. 24) *for why focus it*: Beckett added the interrogative phrase after the text's appearance in *Evergreen*. There the sentence reads *Most of the time I looked up at the sky, but without focussing it*. All American

printings use the alternative *ss* orthography in the participle. *Nouvelles* (p. 99) reads *Je regardais vers le ciel la plupart du temps, mais sans le fixer.*
(p. 25) *up to the age of seventy*: *Nouvelles* (p. 100) reads *On peut se branler jusqu'à la cinquantaine.* It is evident that Beckett, subsequent to 1946, revised his expectations of physiological possibilities.
(p. 25) *up to the knuckle*: Grove 67 and Gontarski 95 agree on a variant reading – *It was in the arse I had the most pleasure. I stuck my forefinger up to the knuckle.* This mirrors the punctuation of the original: *C'était dans le cul que j'avais le plus de satisfaction. J'y enfournais l'index, jusqu'à la métacarpe.* (*Nouvelles*, pp. 100–101.)
(p. 25) *the legs of my trousers all wet*: American printings, with the exception of Gontarski 95, read *leg*.
(p. 26) *bread and butter*: *Nouvelles* (p. 102) reads *bifteck*.
(p. 26) *The voice, God forbid*: Beckett's translation differs substantially from his original at this point – *Réfléchissez-vous? La voix, Non. Bien sûr que non, reprit l'orateur, ça fait partie du décor.*
(p. 27) *The gates were locked and the paths overgrown with grass*: American printings offer a variant reading – *The gates were locked and the paths were overgrown with grass.*
(p. 29) *I was all right, yes, quite so*: *Evergreen* gives *precisely* at this point.
(p. 31) *I swallowed my calmative*: *Evergreen* gives *sedative* at this point. Interestingly, the manuscript copy of the novella *The Calmative* held at Washington University, St Louis, was titled 'The Sedative' at first but altered to *The Calmative* by Beckett.

The Expelled

(p. 32) *with your foot on the sidewalk*: All English language printings of the text credit the translation to 'Richard Seaver in collaboration with the author'. Beckett chose not to 'localize' his text while revising by translating the French original *le trottoir* as *the footpath* for British publication, preferring to keep faith with the American *the sidewalk* throughout, as he had in *The End*.

(p. 35) *and vanish in the air more sorrowful than the neighbours'*: *Evergreen* offers *melancholy* here.

(p. 36) *but the limits of vision itself*: *Evergreen* continues, *That is why I always raise my eyes, in times of great trouble, to this sky which is such a rest, no matter how cloudy, or leaden, or veiled by the rain, from the viewless confusion of the town, the country, the earth. It gets monotonous in the end, but I can't help it.* Grove 67 retains only *It gets monotonous in the end. No's Knife, CSP* and Gontarski 95 omit the passage altogether. The passage is in the original but in a somewhat different order: *C'est ce qui fait que je lève mes yeux, quand tout va mal, c'en est même monotone mais je n'y peux rien, à ce ciel qui repose, même nuageux, même plombé, même voilé par la pluie, du fouillis et de l'aveuglement de la ville, de la campagne, de la terre.* (*Nouvelles*, p. 18.)

(p. 38) *special tracks for these nasty little creatures*: *Evergreen* offers *dirty*.

(p. 38) *but leave some room for others*: The following passage is omitted from the translation – *Je visai sa lèvre supérieure, qui avait au moins trois centimètres de haut, et je soufflai dessus. Je le fis, je crois, avec assez de naturel, comme celui qui, sous la cruelle pression des événements, pousse un profond soupir. Mais il ne broncha pas. Il devait avoir l'habitude des autopsies, ou des exhumations.* (*Nouvelles*, p. 23.)

(p. 39) *the bystanders go their ways*: An earlier version of this clause – *the people come back to life* – appears in *Evergreen*.

(p. 39) *and entered a cab*: *Evergreen* offers *took*.

(p. 39) *when a voice made me start*: *Evergreen* offers *jump*.

(p. 42) *I prefer being with a regular customer in such places*: An earlier version of this sentence – *I'd just as soon be with a regular customer in such places* – appears in *Evergreen*.

(p. 43) *He sang*, She is far from the land where her young hero: The French original (*Nouvelles*, p. 31) offers a straight translation of the whole of the first line in Thomas Moore's poem: *Elle est loin du pays où son jeune héros dort* (She is far from the land where her young hero sleeps). The poem is from Moore's *Irish Melodies* (1808–34); the complete text is most conveniently available in *The Field Day Anthology of Irish Writing, Vol. 1*, edited by Seamus Deane (Field Day Publications, Derry, 1991), p. 1059.

(p. 43) *I was sick and tired of this cabman*: *Evergreen* offers an earlier version of this sentence – *I was beginning to have my bellyful of this cabman*.
(p. 46) *Weakness*: *Evergreen* offers *Weariness*.

The Calmative

(p. 47) *The Calmative*: The title is centred, revised and underlined in the Ms. What Beckett first wrote is manually cancelled but legible as *The Sedative*. The noun is heavily cancelled and *Calmative* inserted above.
(p. 48) *in which I became what I was*: *Nouvelles* (p. 41) has an additional sentence omitted in translation – *Ah je vous en foutrai des temps, salauds de votre temps*. Ms offers *Ah I'll give you times and* [illegible word], the whole phrase cancelled with a horizontal line. This is followed by *Ah je vous foutrai (in)*. Ts 1 has *Ah je vous foutrai*. . . (ellipsis in text) which is again cancelled. The sentence is omitted in Ts 2.
(p. 49) *the crabs never get there too soon*: *Nouvelles* (p. 42) has an additional sentence omitted in translation – *Tout cela est affaire d'organisation*. Ms offers *It's all a question of organisation*. The sentence appears in that form in Ts 1 but is cancelled with a horizontal line. It is omitted from Ts 2.
(p. 49) *A lush pasture lay before me, nonsuch perhaps*: Beckett twice imported the word *minette* from his French original into both Ms and Ts 1: in the latter he substituted the English *nonsuch* while revising and this in turn is what appears in Ts 2. The second occurrence will be duly noted below.
(p. 50) *older than I shall ever be*: *Nouvelles* (p. 45) has an additional sentence – *Me voilà acculé à des futurs*. Ms reads *Look at me now reduced to futures*. Ts 1 reads *There I am reduced to futures*. This is manually cancelled and omitted from Ts 2.
(p. 53) *would come upon that gallows night and*: *Nouvelles* (p. 51) has *cette joyeuse nuit* which is translated in Ms as *joyous* [heavily cancelled followed by illegible word] *gallous evening*. Ts 1 has *gallous* with the *u* manually altered to *w*. Ts 2 has *gallows*.

(p. 54) *if he had given me the chance*: *Nouvelles* (p. 52) continues, *Je suivis du regard les pattes de derrière de la chèvre, décharnées, cagneuses, écartées, secouées de brusques révoltes*. Ms reads *I followed with my eyes the hindlegs of the goat, scraggy, knock kneed, sprawling, ? with obstreperous jerks* (interrogative in Ms). Ts 1 reads *I followed with my eyes the hindlegs of the goat, scraggy, knock-kneed, sprawling,   with obstreperous jerks* (space in Ts1). The passage is cancelled and does not appear in Ts 2.

(p. 54) *I who in the normal way was left standing by cripples*: *Nouvelles* (p. 52) has *les parkinsoniens*, rendered in Ms as *parkinsonians*. This is carried over to Ts 1 where it is manually cancelled and *cripples* interlineally inserted above the cancelled word.

(p. 59) *I longed for the tender nonsuch*: Ms reads *I mourned the tender minette*. Ts 1 offers the same but *mourned* and *minette* are cancelled and *longed for* and *nonsuch* inserted manually.

(p. 60) *I put it back*: This sentence first appears in Ts 2. *Nouvelles* (p. 64) reads *Il réfléchit, c'était un pondéré*. Ms and Ts 1 both offer *He took thought, he was a thinker*. Ts 2 omits that sentence.

(p. 61) *and the streets come to life*: *Nouvelles* (p. 66) continues, *Tu demanderas ton chemin, à un sergent de ville s'il le faut, il sera obligé de te renseigner, sous peine de manquer à son serment*. The Ms version reads *You'll ask your way, of a policeman if necessary* [cancelled] *need be* [substituted interlineally], *he will have to direct you if he doesn't want to break his oath*. Ts 1 offers the same passage but it is lightly cancelled and does not appear in Ts 2.

(p. 62) *like the young woman in the street*: *Nouvelles* (p. 67) continues, *Sur la chèvre aussi ma pensée glissa désolée, impuissante à s'arrêter*. Ms reads *Over the goat too my thought slipped desolate, powerless to grasp*. Ts 1 revises *thought* to *thoughts* and then cancels the sentence.

(p. 62) *in spite of shutters, blinds and muslins*: *Nouvelles* (p. 68) has *les volets, stores et mystères*. Ms renders this as *shutters, blinds and mystères*. Ts 1 similarly, but *mystères* is cancelled and *muslins* substituted interlineally.

(p. 63) *I had no need to raise my head from the ground*: *Nouvelles* (p. 69) has *l'asphalte*: Ms, Ts 1 and Ts 2 give *asphalt*. In Ts 2 this is overtyped and *ground* is typed in the left margin.

(p. 63) *down on the friendly stone*: *Nouvelles* (p. 69) reads *sur ces dalles amicales*. Ms and Ts 1 have *on the friendly flags* but the latter has *flags* manually cancelled and *stones* inserted interlineally. The final version appears in Ts 2.
(p. 63) *don't open your eyes, wait for morning*: *Nouvelles* (p. 69) differs – *n'ouvre pas les yeux, attends que vienne le Samaritain, ou que vienne le jour et avec lui les sergents de ville ou qui sait un salutiste*. Ms and Ts 1 read *wait for the Samaritan to come, or dawn, and with it the police constable or, who knows, a member of the Salvation Army*. Ts 1, however, cancels the passage and substitutes *wait for morning*.

First Love

(p. 64) *on other levels*: Grove 74 offers *on other planes*. Minuit 70 reads *sur d'autres plans*. Here and at other points (which will be duly noted) Grove 74 offers readings based on Ts 2. It is evident, therefore, that Beckett revised the text again prior to first British publication in Calder 73.
(p. 64) *will not easily erase*: In Ms Beckett rendered his original *effacer* as *efface* but inscribed *erase* alongside in the left margin. He opted for *erase* from Ts 1 onwards.
(p. 64) *no bone to pick with graveyards*: Grove 74 offers *Personally I have nothing against graveyards*. This is the wording in Ms, Ts 1 and Ts 2.
(p. 65) *what the living emit*: In the pre-publication documents Beckett hesitated between *sent*, *emit*, *exhale* before finally opting for *emit*.
(p. 65) *the flat, the leaning and the upright*: In reviewing his Ms translation Beckett inscribed a revised wording on the reverse of the final folio: *among the stones, flat, leaning upright* and then inserted a caret in front of each of the adjectivals and wrote the definite article above each one. That complex revision was then incorporated into Ts 1. Ts 2 finalized the wording by substituting *slabs* for *stones* and inserting *and* before *the upright*.

(p. 65) *my epitaph still meets with my approval*: A sentence is omitted here in the translation – *Elle illustre un point de grammaire*. The omission was made by Beckett on the basis of simple relevance.
(p. 65) *that he lived on till now*: Grove 74 offers the version of the epitaph that appears in Ts 2 –

> *Hereunder lies the above who up below*
> *So hourly died that he survived till now.*

(p. 65) *the odd relict trying to throw herself*: Grove 74 offers *rearing*. It is probable that Beckett revised this to *trying* because of his use, earlier in the paragraph and in connection with the epitaph, of the phrase *There is little chance unfortunately of its ever being reared above the skull that conceived it*. In making the revision for Calder 73 Beckett sacrificed numerous punning possibilities: *to rear* may mean *to raise* (as from the dead) and in Hiberno-English usage *rearing* expresses great desire and is in exact parallel to *dying to*.
(p. 66) *unless he happened to have died*: The reading here concurs with *CSP* and Gontarski 95. Calder 73 and Grove 74 offer *unless he happen to have died*. The error arose in Ts 2 where Beckett mistyped. An attempted correction was made for *Four Novellas* (Calder 77) but materialized as *unless he happed to have died*.
(p. 66) *their little gimmick with the dust*: Beckett initially translated his original *cette petite comédie* as *their little game* but opted for *their little gimmick* from Ts 1.
(p. 66) *was not amongst my favourites*: Both Calder 73 and Grove 74 offer *among my favourite*. *CSP* offers *amongst my favourite*. Gontarski 95 offers *amongst my favourites* and that reading is accepted here because conventional usage favours a plural noun following the preposition *amongst*.
(p. 66) *offer consolation*: Grove 74 offers *purvey*.
(p. 66) *and for food to be brought me there*: The preposition *for* is supplied here from Grove 74 and Gontarski 95.
(p. 66) *opposed my eviction*: Ts 1 reads *my being thrown out* with *my eviction* inserted interlinearly; *my eviction* was opted for in Ts 2.

(p. 67) *your home is here*: Minuit 70 offers an additional untranslated sentence – *C'était une maison énorme*.

(p. 67) *on my return from stool*: Minuit 70 is a little less specific – *en revenant des w.-c.*,.

(p. 67) *a bearded stripling in the midst of sheep*: Minuit 70 reads *on y voyait l'image en couleurs d'un jeune homme barbu entouré de moutons*. Ts 1 reads *just gazed dully at the almanac hanging from a nail before my eyes with its coloured print depicting a bearded stripling*. The phrase *coloured print depicting* is struck out and *chromo of* is interlinearly inserted. In the left margin beside *before my eyes* Beckett inscribed the word *forenenst*. Additionally, he carried this suggested substitution over to the reverse of the final folio (folio 15) of Ts 1, where he charted a set of changes, many of which he effected in Ts 2, but not this one.

(p. 67) *Or am I confusing it with diarrhoea?*: Minuit 70 reads *Ou est-ce que je confonds avec la diarrhée?*. The definite article appears before the noun in Calder 73 and Grove 74; it was deleted for *CSP*.

(p. 68) *nothing less than gas would have dislodged me*: Minuit 70 reads *seuls les gaz m'en auraient fait sortir*. Both Ts 2 and Grove 74 offer *they would have had to gas me out*. Beckett made the revision for Calder 73.

(p. 68) *the fumigation can wait*: Again, the original is a little less specific – *la chambre peut attendre*.

(p. 69) *Of course one can never tell*: Minuit 70 contains a passage omitted from the published English language editions and Ts 2, but included in Ms and Ts 1 – *N'étant pas française elle disait Loulou. Moi aussi, n'étant pas français non plus, je disais Loulou comme elle. Tous les deux, nous disions Loulou*. Ms reads *Not being French she pronounced* [cancelled] *said Loulou. I too, not being French either, said Loulou. We both said Loulou*.

(p. 69) *I hate to forget a proper name*: Ts 2 and Grove 74 offer *I hate forgetting a proper name*.

(p. 69) *All she had done was sing*: Ts 2 and Grove 74 read *All she had done was sing*, sotto voce, *as to herself*,. The punctuation printed here is that of Calder 73 and *CSP*; Gontarski 95 differs slightly.

(p. 70) *mine own, the mitigable*: In Ts 1 Beckett hesitated between *bridled*, *manageable* and *mitigable*, finally opting for the last, which was carried over to Ts 2.
(p. 71) *it was alone*: Minuit 70 reads *je me trouvai seul.*
(p. 71) *my mean soul*: Minuit 70 reads *mon âme bourgeoise.*
(p. 71) *no more tattle about that*: Ts 1 reads *old guff* which is struck out and *tattle* sustituted.
(p. 72) *trench foot and other curiosities*: This listing is a considerable amplification of the original Minuit 70 – *et sans me presser jusqu'aux pieds, siège des cors, crampes, oignons, ongles incarnés, trenchfoot et autres bizarreries.*
(p. 73) *if I had not to husband my cyanide*: Minuit 70 has *morphine.*
(p. 73) *at home, in school, in brothel and at church*: *CSP* is the only English language edition to vary the symmetrical pattern of the prepositions – *at . . . in . . . in . . . at* to *at . . . at . . . in . . . at.*
(p. 73) *in which it was handled at length*: Beckett's translation departs significantly from his original version in Minuit 70 – *et j'avais lu des romans, en prose et en vers, sous la direction de mon tuteur, en anglais, en français, en italien, en allemand, où il en était fortement question.*
(p. 74) *I'll give her another, more like her, Anna*: In Minuit 70 the alternative name given is *Anne*. Curiously, the alternative given in Ms and Ts 1 is *Oona*. Beckett did not settle for the alternative *Anna* until Ts 2.
(p. 75) *in time's forgotten cowpats?*: Calder 73 and Grove 74 offer *cowplats*. Beckett marked the change to *cowpats* on a set of corrected proofs for *CSP* (in the possession of Mr Glenn Horowitz). Minuit 70 reads: *Car, si je l'avais aimée de cette manière, est-ce que je me serais amusé à tracer le mot Anne sur d'immémoriaux excréments de bovin?* Beckett's Ms reads – *For had my love been of this kind, would I have stooped to trace the letters* [cancelled] *name of Oona on immemorial bovine excrement?* This was revised in Ts 1 to . . . *to inscribe the letters of Oona in immemorial bovine excrement?* The final three words were then underlined and *claps of vanished kine* inserted in the left margin. A further revision, . . . *to inscribe the letters of Anna in time's forgotten cowplats*, is effected in Ts 2. Both *cowplat* and *cowclap* are listed in *OED* (first edition) so it would seem that Beckett's late revision in

proof for *CSP* was motivated by the desire to connect with the reference earlier in the text to *inscribing the letters of Lulu in an old heifer pat*.

(p. 77) *even more dead than alive than usual*: Beckett's translation offers an intensification of his original *plus mort que vif*.

(p. 77) *But why these particulars?*: The interrogative is missing from all British editions of the text but appears in Minuit 70 and Grove 74. Ms and Ts 1 read *But why these details?* This was revised to *But why these particulars?* in Ts 2 but the curve of the interrogative overruns the right edge of the paper and is therefore only partially visible.

(p. 79) *perhaps it was the shorter way*: The wording here is from Calder 73 and *CSP*.

(p. 79) *There were hundreds of pieces*: The reading here is from *CSP* and restores the reading of Ts 1. Earlier British and American printings read *They were hundreds*. . . The error arose from Beckett's mistyping in Ts 2.

(p. 79) *but had become impassable*: Minuit 70 differs on the subject of the door – *mais elle était devenue infranchissable. Un bien grand mot, infranchissable*.

(p. 80) *I heard the word fibrome, or brone*: Minuit 70 differs – *j'entendis le mot fibrome ou fibrone*.

(p. 80) *Give me a chamber-pot, I said*: Minuit 70 continues, *J'ai beaucoup aimé, pendant assez longtemps, les mots vase de nuit, ils me faisaient penser à Racine, ou à Baudelaire, je ne sais plus lequel, aux deux peut-être, oui, je regrette, j'avais de la lecture, et par eux j'arrivais là où le verbe s'arrête, on dirait du Dante*.

(p. 80) *I don't have the flux*: Minuit 70 has *la dysenterie*. Ms and Ts 1 read *I don't have dysentery*. The final version first appears in Ts 2.

(p. 80) *My stewpan, she said*: Minuit 70 has *le faitout*.

(p. 81) *and vent some phrase or phrases*: Grove 74 has *void*.

(p. 81) *Why behind her?*: This question is an addition to the English language text; it does not appear in Minuit 70.

(p. 82) *Not a day passed without my looking at it*: Minuit 70 is more specific regarding this hyacinth – *Elle était rose. J'aurais préféré une bleue*.

(p. 83) *feed me nothing but parsnips I'd be grateful*: Minuit 70 has an additional, untranslated sentence – *Que de panais! s'écria-t-elle*.
(p. 83) *Perhaps it's just wind*: Grove 74 has *mere*.

READ MORE IN PENGUIN

In every corner of the world, on every subject under the sun, Penguin represents quality and variety – the very best in publishing today.

For complete information about books available from Penguin – including Puffins, Penguin Classics and Arkana – and how to order them, write to us at the appropriate address below. Please note that for copyright reasons the selection of books varies from country to country.

In the United Kingdom: Please write to *Dept. EP, Penguin Books Ltd, Bath Road, Harmondsworth, West Drayton, Middlesex UB7 0DA*

In the United States: Please write to *Consumer Services, Penguin Putnam Inc., 405 Murray Hill Parkway, East Rutherford, New Jersey 07073-2136.* VISA and MasterCard holders call 1-800-631-8571 to order Penguin titles

In Canada: Please write to *Penguin Books Canada Ltd, 10 Alcorn Avenue, Suite 300, Toronto, Ontario M4V 3B2*

In Australia: Please write to *Penguin Books Australia Ltd, 487 Maroondah Highway, Ringwood, Victoria 3134*

In New Zealand: Please write to *Penguin Books (NZ) Ltd, Private Bag 102902, North Shore Mail Centre, Auckland 10*

In India: Please write to *Penguin Books India Pvt Ltd, 11 Community Centre, Panchsheel Park, New Delhi 110017*

In the Netherlands: Please write to *Penguin Books Netherlands bv, Postbus 3507, NL-1001 AH Amsterdam*

In Germany: Please write to *Penguin Books Deutschland GmbH, Metzlerstrasse 26, 60594 Frankfurt am Main*

In Spain: Please write to *Penguin Books S. A., Bravo Murillo 19, 1°B, 28015 Madrid*

In Italy: Please write to *Penguin Italia s.r.l., Via Vittorio Emanuele 45/a, 20094 Corsico, Milano*

In France: Please write to *Penguin France, 12, Rue Prosper Ferradou, 31700 Blagnac*

In Japan: Please write to *Penguin Books Japan Ltd, Iidabashi KM-Bldg, 2-23-9 Koraku, Bunkyo-Ku, Tokyo 112-0004*

In South Africa: Please write to *Penguin Books South Africa (Pty) Ltd, P.O. Box 751093, Gardenview, 2047 Johannesburg*

READ MORE IN PENGUIN

Published or forthcoming:

Swann's Way Marcel Proust

This first book of Proust's supreme masterpiece, *A la recherche du temps perdu*, recalls the early youth of Charles Swann in the small, provincial backwater of Combray through the eyes of the adult narrator. The story then moves forward to Swann's life as a man of fashion in the glittering world of *belle-époque* Paris. A scathing, often comic dissection of French society, *Swann's Way* is also a story of past moments tantalizingly lost and, finally, triumphantly rediscovered.

Metamorphosis and Other Stories Franz Kafka

A companion volume to *The Great Wall of China and Other Short Works*, these translations bring together the small proportion of Kafka's works that he thought worthy of publication. This volume contains his most famous story, 'Metamorphosis'. All the stories reveal the breadth of Kafka's literary vision and the extraordinary imaginative depth of his thought.

Cancer Ward Aleksandr Solzhenitsyn

One of the great allegorical masterpieces of world literature, *Cancer Ward* is both a deeply compassionate study of people facing terminal illness and a brilliant dissection of the 'cancerous' Soviet police state. Withdrawn from publication in Russia in 1964, it became a work that awoke the conscience of the world. 'Without doubt the greatest Russian novelist of this century' *Sunday Times*

Peter Camenzind Hermann Hesse

In a moment of 'emotion recollected in tranquility' Peter Camenzind recounts the days of his youth: his childhood in a remote mountain village, his abiding love of nature, and the discovery of literature which inspires him to leave the village and become a writer. 'One of the most penetrating accounts of a young man trying to discover the nature of his creative talent' *The Times Literary Supplement*